Acting Edition

The Mad Ones

by Kait Kerrigan
and Bree Lowdermilk

CONCORD
THEATRICALS

FOR PRODUCTION INQUIRIES

UNITED STATES AND CANADA
info@concordtheatricals.com
1-866-979-0447

UNITED KINGDOM AND EUROPE
licensing@concordtheatricals.co.uk
020-7054-7200

Each title is subject to availability from Concord Theatricals Corp.,
depending upon country of performance. Please be aware that *THE
MAD ONES* may not be licensed by Concord Theatricals Corp. in
your territory. Professional and amateur producers should contact the
nearest Concord Theatricals Corp. office or licensing partner to verify
availability.

---

system, scanned, uploaded, or transmitted in any form, by any means, now known or yet to be invented, including mechanical, electronic, digital, photocopying, recording, videotaping, or otherwise, without the prior written permission of the publisher. No one shall share this title(s), or any part of this title(s), through any social media or file hosting websites.

For all inquiries regarding motion picture, television, online/digital and other media rights, please contact Concord Theatricals Corp.

MUSIC AND THIRD-PARTY MATERIALS USE NOTE

Licensees are solely responsible for obtaining formal written permission from copyright owners to use copyrighted music and/or other copyrighted third-party materials (e.g., artworks, logos) in the performance of this play and are strongly cautioned to do so. If no such permission is obtained by the licensee, then the licensee must use only original music and materials that the licensee owns and controls. Licensees are solely responsible and liable for clearances of all third-party copyrighted materials, including without limitation music, and shall indemnify the copyright owners of the play(s) and their licensing agent, Concord Theatricals Corp., against any costs, expenses, losses and liabilities arising from the use of such copyrighted third-party materials by licensees. For music, please contact the appropriate music licensing authority in your territory for the rights to any incidental music.

IMPORTANT BILLING AND CREDIT REQUIREMENTS

If you have obtained performance rights to this title, please refer to your licensing agreement for important billing and credit requirements.

THE MAD ONES was based on an idea by Zach Altman and Bree Lowdermilk. The New York premiere was produced by Prospect Theater Company in New York, New York on November 7, 2017; Cara Reichel, Producing Artistic Director Melissa Huber, Managing Director. Originally produced by Goodspeed Musicals; Michael P. Price, Executive Producer. Presented at the National Alliance for Musical Theatre's Festival of New Musicals in 2016.

The Prospect Theater Company production was directed by Stephen Brackett with choreography by Alexandra Beller, sets by Adam Rigg, costumes by Jessica Pabst, lights by David Lander, sound by Alex Hawthorn, electronic music design by Dana Haynes, and orchestrations by Bree Lowdermilk. The music director was Paul Staroba, the associate music director was Jeremy Robin Lyons, the production stage manager was Veronica Aglow, and the assistant stage manager was Jenna R. Lazar. The opening night cast was as follows:

SAM . . . . Krystina Alabado
KELLY . . . . Emma Huton
BEVERLY . . . . Leah Hocking
ADAM . . . . Jay Armstrong Johnson
UNDERSTUDY SAM / KELLY . . . . Melissa Rose Hirsch

SONG LIST

"The Girl Who Drove Away" . . . . **SAM**
"Freedom" . . . . **SAM, KELLY**
"My Mom is a Statistician" . . . . **SAM, BEVERLY**
"Sam Failed Her Driver's Test". . . . . **SAM, KELLY, BEVERLY, ADAM**
"Top Ten". . . . . **SAM, KELLY**
"Simple as That". . . . . **SAM, ADAM**
"The Proposal" . . . . **SAM, KELLY, BEVERLY, ADAM**
"The Mad Ones". . . . . **SAM, KELLY**
"I Know My Girl". . . . . **BEVERLY, SAM, KELLY, ADAM**
"Miles to Go". . . . . **BEVERLY**
"Say The Word" . . . . **SAM, ADAM**
"Moving On". . . . . **SAM, KELLY, BEVERLY, ADAM**
"Go Tonight". . . . . **SAM, KELLY**
"Run Away With Me" . . . . **ADAM**
"Drive" . . . . **SAM, KELLY, BEVERLY, ADAM**
"I Didn't Say Goodbye". . . . . **KELLY**
"Remember This". **SAM, KELLY, ADAM, BEVERLY**

CHARACTERS

SAM – (18) Smart, with a wry sense of humor and wicked sense of play. She takes herself too seriously. She is a worrier. Detached and straight-forward but it would be wise to cast against type. The actress needs to access a deep reservoir of emotion. She must transform into the star of the show. Witnessing that metamorphosis is the theatrical purpose of the evening. The part requires an infinitely inventive and exciting actress. In other words, don't let Kelly fool you: Sam is the star.

KELLY – (18) So alive, spontaneous, brighter than bright, cooler than cool. She is not bookish like Sam but she has intuition and a deep ability to connect with the human condition.

BEVERLY – (Early 50s) Sam's mother. A professor of statistics. Incisive, dead pan. Previously remote, Bev's been more involved of late – one might say overbearing.

ADAM – (18) Kind, a heartthrob. He has great emotional intelligence and the loyalty of a St. Bernard.

SETTING

The set must allow for great transformation with small elegant gestures. Moments should appear and disappear with the speed and fluidity of a mind's eye. Better for it to be a blank stage with a single chair than naturalistic.

TIME

THE MAD ONES takes place in a flash – within the seconds it would take to turn the key in the ignition of a car. But as we all know, those seconds can expand or contract especially when fear seizes you up and makes you forget how you got here. So, you have to remind yourself. This play is a reminder.

AUTHORS' NOTES

THE MAD ONES is intended to be performed in one. Scenes flow seamlessly as they do in memory – one into another. There is no intermission and it runs about ninety minutes.

When we did the show Off-Broadway in a small venue, we opted for no applause until the very end of the performance (letting the tension build more like a play than like it does as a musical). We recognize that there might be productions that may benefit from certain numbers having "buttons." (If you use hydraulics during "The Proposal," the audience is going to want to applaud after all. Kidding / not kidding.) In such key songs, we've included notes in the footer on how to implement buttons or frustrate applause accordingly.

Beats and pauses should be observed. Ellipses (...) indicate that the actor should trail off and en dashes (–) indicate that a character is cut off by the following line.

I.

["THE GIRL WHO DROVE AWAY"]

(Lights rise on **SAM.***)*

SAM.

IT STARTS AS NOTHING,
JUST A THOUGHT OR A DREAM.
THEN ONE DAY YOU'RE IN THE DRIVER'S SEAT,
THE KEY IS IN THE IGNITION,
AND NO ONE GAVE YOU PERMISSION.
IT'S ONLY YOU IN THE CAR
AND ONLY YOU KNOW HOW UNCERTAIN YOUR ARE,
HOW YOUR HEART IS RACING.
STILL YOU REACH FOR THE MOMENT
YOU'LL FINALLY SAY,
I'M THE GIRL WHO DROVE AWAY.

LEAVE THE FEAR AND DOUBT BEHIND.
CHOOSE THE ROAD LESS TRAVELED,
NOT THE MEM'RIES TOO REAL,
NOT THE GUILT THAT LEFT YOU PARALYZED.
CLOSE YOUR EYES, AND EVERYTHING'S CLEARER.
YOUR LIFE'S IN THE REAR VIEW MIRROR.
IF NO ONE KNOWS WHO YOU WERE,
THE LINE BETWEEN THE DREAM AND YOU
STARTS TO BLUR.
STANDING AT THE CROSSROAD:
THERE'S THE GIRL WHO WAS WRITTEN IN YOUR DNA,
OR THE GIRL WHO DROVE AWAY.

IF I COULD FEEL IT:
THE WAY THE DAY BLOWS ACROSS THE SKY,
AND HOW THE MILES KEEP ON FLYING BY.
THE DAWN IS BREAKING,

THE SUN'S NEARLY WAKING THE LIFE INSIDE ME...

IF ONLY I COULD TURN THE KEY.

> (*A moment passes. She holds the key in her hand. Can she turn it in the ignition?*)
>
> (*She stops. She second guesses.*)
>
> (*The subtle sounds of suburban life. Sprinklers, cars passing, maybe a lawn mower.*)"

> (**KELLY** *appears.*)

KELLY. I knew you'd choke.

SAM. Kelly?! What are you –

KELLY. Chill. I'm like your cautious.

SAM. My – conscience?

KELLY. *No.* Your *cautious*. Like when some dude tries to bareball it and you're like, "Maybe..." But then your *cautious* is like, "NO! What are you thinking? That boy might be nasty," and so you don't.

SAM. Kelly, I'm freaking out.

KELLY. Where you headed?

SAM. I don't know. It's not like I have a map or anything.

KELLY. Well. Maps are for brain deads.

SAM. I was just daydreaming.

KELLY. Technically, you still are.

SAM. You're not here.

KELLY. Aren't I?

SAM. No. I'm sitting alone in a parked car –

KELLY. My car.

> (*Beat.*)

SAM. Yeah.

> (*Resuming.*)

I'm sitting alone in your car in my mother's driveway at dawn –

KELLY. Talking to yourself.

SAM. Yeah. I need to go back inside.

KELLY. Fine. Go.

SAM. I'm supposed to leave for college today.

KELLY. Go!

SAM. I'm the valedictorian. The valedictorian goes to college.

KELLY. Oh *I* know.

SAM. But what if –

KELLY. What if she doesn't? Oh, twist.

(*Memories swell up around* **SAM.**)

ADAM.	**BEVERLY.**	**KELLY.**	**SAM.**
HEY SAM,	SLIDE THE CAR INTO GEAR,	LET'S GO	REMEMBER
I WAS WONDERING	EASE YOUR FOOT OFF THE BRAKE.	LET'S GO	REMEMBER...
WOULD YOU BE MY DATE	THAT'S IT.		
TO THE FRESHMAN FLING?	THAT'S ALL IT IS.		
HEY, SAM.	NOW YOU LET IT GO.		

KELLY. YO! Snap out of it.

(*Memories burst like a soap bubble and are gone.*)

SAM. Sorry. I think of one memory and they all come flooding back in a big jumble.

KELLY. (*Mocking.*) Not a memory jumble.

SAM. Shut up.

KELLY. Is this about that book?

SAM. What?

KELLY. That book you're always talking about. *On the Highway*? *On the Dirt*?

(**KELLY** *digs through* **SAM***'s backpack.*)

SAM. *On the Road*?

KELLY. Tell me this is not about a book.

SAM. It's not about a book.

KELLY. OK because I read that book *for you* and those guys were, like, as high as kites and the whole thing literally is like just boys, driving, on a road.

SAM. I think you only read the first five pages.

KELLY. What does your mom think of that book?

BEVERLY. (*Appearing.*) *On the Road* is what happens when you glorify the patriarchy.

SAM. Oh God! Make her go away.

KELLY. Think about Adam.

ADAM. (*Appearing.*) Why'd you break up with me?

SAM. Funny.

(*They disappear.*)

KELLY. Right?

SAM. This is your fault. All of this. I was figuring out who I was – the whole year – saying what I wanted, *doing* it, and then one day the phone rings –

(*A memory flashes. The sound of a distant phone ringing.* **KELLY** *in another time and place. One of those moments that just sticks to your brain matter.*)

KELLY. (*Out of context, distinctive.*)
WHAT – YOU THINK IT'S GONNA BITE?

(*A moment passes.* **SAM** *is lost in her own thoughts.*)

SAM. (*To audience.*) Kelly and I – we were –. Kelly was the kind of friend who would ghost for days and then show up in your driveway like nothing happened. She didn't have a cell phone. She lived for –

KELLY. What is this?

SAM. I'm – contextualizing.

KELLY. To who – to me?

SAM. I hate you.

KELLY. You love me. And whatever, I called you all the time.

SAM. Yeah. From some random number with frat boys screaming in the background.

KELLY. You never picked up.

SAM. Text me like a normal person!

KELLY. I don't *type*. I'm not a secretary.

SAM. Kelly –

KELLY. What do you want, Sam?

SAM. I don't remember anymore.

KELLY. OK. Give me the keys.

SAM. What?

KELLY. Get in the car, loser.

> *(Chord.* **KELLY** *takes the keys from* **SAM**.*)*

SAM. What are you doing?

KELLY. Contextualizing! Think about the one time I got you to skip school. Fall of senior year.

SAM. No.

KELLY. You said no then too. I said, "Get in, loser, you're wasting your best life."

> *(Chord.)*

SAM. I won't.

KELLY. I said, "Samantha Brown. Get in the car."

SAM. I can't do this.

> *(Chord.)*

["FREEDOM"]

KELLY.
LET'S GO!
THE HIGHWAY'S CALLING.
THE SUN IS SHINING.

LET'S GET IN THE CAR AND JUST REMEMBER.
LET'S GO.

    (Flashback.)

KELLY. Get in, loser!

    *(**SAM** gets in the car.)*

SAM. *(Explaining, a little uncomfortable.)*
KELLY DROVE ON ALL OF OUR ROAD TRIPS.
SHE BELIEVED IN LIST'NING TO THE HIGHWAY.
YOU START DRIVING,
AND KEEP DRIVING.
THERE'S NO STOPPING
'TIL KELLY SAYS YOU'VE ARRIVED.

KELLY. *(Stage aside.)* You're not doing it right.

SAM. Doing what?

KELLY. You're not *in it*.

SAM. What are you talking about?

KELLY. You're not in the moment, Sam. Talk about what it *felt* like.

SAM. What did it *feel* like?

KELLY. You remember.
FEELING THE WIND BLOWING YOUR HAIR.
You're not even trying.

SAM. I am.

KELLY. Try harder.
PICKING A ROAD AND GOING ANYWHERE.
Remember the biker bar?

SAM. Oh God.

KELLY.
WE'RE HEADING SOUTH.
And the biker.

    *(**SAM** laughs in spite of herself.)*

OR MAYBE WEST –
WE DON'T KNOW MUCH.
WE'RE MAKING UP THE REST.

TEAR UP THE ATLAS.

DON'T READ THE ROAD SIGNS.

DRIVING FOR THE SAKE OF DRIVING ANYWHERE,

THAT'S FREEDOM.

SAM. *(Half-hearted.)*

FREEDOM.

KELLY. *(In flashback, registering **SAM**'s despondence.)* What bug do you have up your ass?

SAM. I don't have a bug up my ass!

KELLY. *(New tactic.)* Samantha Brown. Do you see that fork up ahead?

SAM. Yeah.

KELLY. Well, one way leads to our school and the other leads somewhere else. Which way do you want to turn? Left or right.

SAM. I don't know. You never take the same route twice. I have no idea where we are.

KELLY. Who cares? If you don't choose, we're gonna hit that house. Left or right!

SAM. Hold on – let me pull up a map.

KELLY. Maps are for brain deads! Left or right?!

SAM. Ah… Left!

> *(**KELLY** turns the car fast, a near miss. A horn honks. She flips the loser off.)*

KELLY. Very slow, Brown.

SAM. So where are we going?

KELLY. I have no idea.

> *(**SAM** wants to be mad but she can't be. She laughs. Something wound up inside her releases.)*

COUNTING THE MILES AS WE GO PAST.

SAM.

THE TANK IS FULL. THE SUN IS HIGH.

KELLY.

KNOWING THAT EVERY MILE COULD BE OUR LAST,

SAM.
>JUST WATCHING THE DAY GO BY.

SAM & KELLY.
>WE WON'T LOOK BACK.
>WE NEVER WILL.

KELLY.
>WE'VE COME TOO FAR.

SAM.
>WE'LL DRIVE 'TIL WE HIT NASHVILLE.

KELLY.
>NASHVILLE!

SAM & KELLY.
>FREEDOM.
>FREEDOM.
>FREEDOM.

KELLY. OK. What do you want to do now?

SAM. *(Confident.)* Make a right.

KELLY. In life, Sam. Think big. What do you *want*?

SAM. Ugh I don't know. I want to get my license.

KELLY. Bigger.

SAM. I want the deafening sound of driving fast with the windows down.

KELLY. More!

SAM. I want to break rules and do something unexpected.

KELLY. Good. I want Arby's.

SAM. I want to reach the horizon of impossibility.

KELLY. I want to go skinny-dipping in the ocean.

SAM. I want to drive forever!

AND I'M ALMOST	
STARTING TO FEEL IT,	**KELLY.**
HOW A DAY GIVES WAY	FREEDOM.
TO SOMETHING DEEPER.	
THE CHEAP REST STOP,	
THE TOWN BY-PASSED,	FREEDOM.
THE LAST MINUTE	

GET IN THE CAR
AND LET'S GO.

KELLY.

OH, LET'S GO.
LET'S GO.
PICK A ROAD. PICK A HIGHWAY.
ANY ROAD IS GOING MY WAY.
LET'S GO.
LIVE IT UP WITH NO COMPLICATED PHILOSOPHIES.
NO COLLEGE, NO CAREER,
NO KIDS, NO FANCY HOUSE, NO.
LET'S GO.
ANY ROAD BUT THE ROAD WE'RE ON.

SAM & KELLY.

NO COLLEGE, NO CAREER,
NO SCREAMING KIDS, NO MORTGAGE.
DRIVING ANYWHERE.

KELLY.

JUST DRIVING STRAIGHT INTO THE DAWN.
THAT'S FREEDOM.

> *(A distant drum beat pulses.)*

SAM.

THERE'S SOMETHING BURIED
WITHIN HERE –
A LESSON TO KEEP.
THE IMPULSE,
THE LIFE FORCE,
THE DIVING IN DEEP.
I FEEL IT,
THE CHAOS I USUALLY FLEE
IF I HOLD ON RIGHT HERE
COULD I LEARN TO JUST – BE?

> *(**SAM** closes her eyes and takes a deep breath –
> willing herself into an awareness that she
> could lose at any moment. She balances on
> an emotional tightrope.)*

(Self-instructing.) Don't talk about it – live it. Don't feel the loss of it feel *it*.

>*(She looks* **KELLY***, who is driving and grooving along to the radio – pure, in flashback – unperturbed by* **SAM***'s present struggle.)*

KELLY DRIVING, ME RIDING SHOTGUN.
Windows open, so loud I can't hear.
JUST A COUPLE GIRLS OUT ON THE HIGHWAY.
Trees blurring into nothing. And I'm nothing. And she's nothing.
THERE'S NO ROAD MAP AND NO CURFEW.
JUST TWO GIRLS WITH NOWHERE WE HAVE TO BE.

>*(***KELLY*** starts singing lightly along with the radio.)*

SAM.	KELLY.
NOW SHE'S LAUGHING.	FREEDOM.
AND I START LAUGHING.	FREEDOM.
IT'S SO REAL	FREEDOM.
AND SO LIKE A MEMORY.	
AND THE SUN	
IS SO BRIGHT	
THAT I'M SQUINTING.	
AND IT FEELS LIKE	
I FOUND FREEDOM.	

SAM & KELLY.

FREEDOM.

SAM.	KELLY.
DRIVING FAST,	YEAH
THE RADIO BLARING	
WINDOWS OPEN,	YEAH
SINGING LIKE	
WE'RE ROCK STARS	

KELLY. *(Riffing.)*

OH YEAH.

>*(She looks at* **SAM***, expectant.)*

SAM. *(Tentative.)*

YEAH.

KELLY.

YEAH.

SAM. *(More confident.)*

YEAH.

KELLY.

YEAH.

SAM. *(With abandon.)*

YEAH.

KELLY. *(Riffing her face off.)*

YEAH.

YEAH.

YEAH.

YEAH.

YEAH.

SAM & KELLY.

FREEDOM.

FREEDOM.

FREEDOM*.

> *(The sound of the car crashing – loud, real, overwhelming. A jolt.)*
>
> *(Then –)*

---

* Option to button. See score. If the song buttons, use the car crash sound effect to cut off the tail end of the applause.

II.

["ORDINARY SENIOR YEAR"]

(Beat. **SAM** *doesn't acknowledge* **KELLY**. *She's in her own world.)*

SAM.

SOMETHING CHANGED.
THE WHOLE WORLD COLLAPSED.
I WAS ON A CERTAIN PATH,
I KNEW WHAT TO DO –
I DON'T KNOW AT ALL NOW.
THE LEAVES START TO TURN –
IT'S FALL NOW.
AM I THAT GIRL ANYMORE?
THAT ORDINARY GIRL THAT I WAS BEFORE?

KELLY.

YOU DON'T HAVE TO KNOW THAT RIGHT NOW.
START AGAIN.
TELL THE STORY OF HOW YOU GOT HERE
FROM AN ORDINARY SENIOR YEAR.
Maybe start with your mom.

*(***BEVERLY*** appears. She clears her throat.)*

SAM. What?

KELLY. Tag out.

SAM. No, no, no, no –

*(***KELLY*** disappears and* **SAM** *is left with her mother.)*

BEVERLY. I knew Samantha was something special when she started reciting passages from my signed copy of the *Second Sex* when she was six.

SAM. Mom.

BEVERLY. *(Ignoring her.)* It didn't occur to me that someone so brilliant could be such a disaster behind the wheel of a car.

SAM. ADAM!!

ADAM. *(Appearing.)* Yeah?

SAM. Did my mother ever haze or intimidate you?

ADAM. Ye –

> *(He looks at **BEVERLY** and changes his mind.)*

no. No. About that – are we still together, technically, or –

BEVERLY. You know, only two percent of high school sweethearts get married.

SAM. Thanks, mom.

BEVERLY. Numbers don't lie.

SAM. It's easy to look at my mom and Adam and say everything was fine. But they both were so *certain*. About everything. About who I was. And I'm – I *wasn't*. I'm not.

> *(**SAM** looks at the key in her hand.)*

My mom was teaching me to drive. And I was struggling. Maybe it was a lack of hand-eye-coordination –

["MY MOM IS A STATISTICIAN"]

BEVERLY. Or maybe it was a healthy respect for the inertia of two tons of steel hurdling into oncoming traffic –

SAM. Or maybe it was the pressure of learning how to drive from the woman who literally wrote the book on driving safety.

> *(**BEVERLY** brandishes a book.)*

BEVERLY. *My Way on the Highway: A Parent's Guide to Driving Safety* by Beverly Brown.

SAM.
MY MOM IS A STATISTICIAN.
AND SHE SEES STATISTICS EVERYWHERE.

BEVERLY.
TWO TO ONE YOU HIT A RED LIGHT.
FIFTY TO ONE YOU HIT A BEAR.

SAM.
SHE SEES THE WORLD AS A HIGH-RISK GAME,

GAMBLING WITH A FANCY NAME,
TRYING TO CHEAT DEATH AND STAY ALIVE.
THIS IS THE WAY SHE TAUGHT ME HOW TO DRIVE.
Observe.

BEVERLY. Say a car is traveling down a road at a constant velocity of 57 miles per hour and a pedestrian is crossing the road at 2.5 miles per hour. If the driver sees the pedestrian from a distance of 132 feet and brakes, decelerating at a rate of 11.1 miles per hour per second, will the car hit the pedestrian? If so, when?

SAM. The answer, obviously, is yes. In 2 seconds. Physics is easy – just plug the right numbers into the equation. Driving is...*real*.

BEVERLY. Are you ready to drive?

SAM. Are you ready for me to drive?

BEVERLY. Sure. I've had a good life.

SAM. Facts about my mom: she got her PhD at twenty-five, tenure at thirty-five, thought, "I want a kid." Had one. Raised me on her own. Stayed out of the way as long as my grades were in check – a move backed by stats. Then, my senior year, she got kind of – mushy.

> (**SAM** *drives. Her mom looks on lovingly.*)

BEVERLY. *(Singing sweetly.)*
SLOW DOWN, SAM.
YOU'RE GROWING UP TOO FAST.
WHEN IT'S TIME TO GO,
I WILL LET YOU KNOW.
I'LL TELL YOU WHEN, SAM.
UNTIL THEN, SAM,
LET'S JUST TAKE THINGS SLOW.

> (*Then, the car lurches.*)

> (*Suddenly, a light switch – Monster Mother.*)

Slow down, Sam! Jesus.
DO YOU KNOW HOW MANY PEOPLE DIE
IN CAR WRECKS EVERY YEAR?

SAM.

YES I DO.

BEVERLY.

YOU DON'T!

SAM.

I DO!

SAM & BEVERLY.

FORTY-ONE THOUSAND PEOPLE –

BEVERLY.

EVERY YEAR –

SAM.

I KNOW!

BEVERLY.

THAT'S A HUNDRED PEOPLE A DAY.

SAM.

MOM.

BEVERLY.

SAM. YOU'LL BE A DEAD MAN –

SAM.

WOMAN.

BEVERLY.

CHILDREN UNDER TWENTY
SHOULDN'T BE ALLOWED TO DRIVE
YOU CAN'T TRUST YOUR FRONTAL CORTEX
IF YOU WANNA STAY ALIVE.
GRIP ON TIGHTER WHEN YOU STEER
AND OVERCOMPENSATE WITH FEAR.
OR YOU WILL DIE TOMORROW.
IN THE MIDDLE OF THE NIGHT,
YOU'LL CRASH AND SKID INTO A DITCH
AND NO ONE WILL BE ABLE TO FIND YOUR
MANGLED
DEAD
CORPSE.

(Beat.)

SAM. Yep. That's the mother I know and love.

BEVERLY.

OOH.

SAM. But OK, here's the thing: I *am* a bad driver. But not because I'm reckless. I just know everything that can go wrong in a car. Thanks, Mom. So every time I get behind the wheel my anxiety becomes this echo chamber of fear and pot holes and squirrels. Turns out, being scared can make you legitimately dangerous.

(**ADAM** *and* **KELLY** *appear.*)

KELLY. Hang on there, Evel Knievel, you weren't that bad.

["SAM FAILED HER DRIVER'S TEST"]

BEVERLY. You want to drive with her?

ADAM. Pass.

SAM. The first time you fail to
get your license: adorable.

KELLY, ADAM & BEVERLY.

The second time: surprising.   OH
But I was ambitious.

KELLY, ADAM & BEVERLY.

SAM FAILED HER
DRIVER'S TEST FOUR
TIMES

SAM. The first time barely counts: I forgot my glasses.

ADAM. Medical condition.

KELLY, ADAM & BEVERLY.

THAT'S ONE!

SAM. Next, a parked car bumped into *me*.

BEVERLY. Divine intervention?

KELLY, ADAM & BEVERLY.

THAT'S TWO! HOO-OO

SAM. The third time, I left the parking brake on, which caused the burning smell, which caused me to panic, which caused me to...

SAM, KELLY, ADAM & BEVERLY.

PEE.
AND FLEE.

SAM, ADAM & BEVERLY.
>THAT'S THREE...

>>*(**KELLY** sits down in a car with a clipboard.)*

KELLY. *(Minnesotan accent.)* Samantha Brown?

KELLY, ADAM & BEVERLY.
>YEAH, SHE FAILED ONE MORE!
>DRIVER'S TEST NUMBER FOUR!

SAM. *(Stage aside.)* Kelly, what are you doing?

KELLY. *(Stage aside.)* Don't talk about it, Sam – live it.

>>*(**SAM** is skeptical.)*

>WATCH FOR TRAFFIC.
The car's not going to drive itself.
>BOTH HANDS ON THE WHEEL.

>>*(Once again, the memory flashes. A distant phone ring. The music shifts. **KELLY** is trapped in a moment.)*

>WHAT – YOU THINK IT'S GONNA BITE?

>>*(**KELLY** looks at her in the present moment expectantly.)*

Well?

SAM. No.

>*(She sits down.)*

KELLY. *(So into it.)* OK. You be Sam.

SAM. Who are you?

KELLY. The DMV lady Carol Ann. She's from Minnesota.

SAM. No, she's isn't.

KELLY. *(As **CAROL ANN**.)* She is now, don'tcha know!
*(Stage aside as **KELLY**.)* Turn the key. What does it feel like?

>>*(**SAM** turns the key in the ignition and the whole world comes to life for **SAM**.)*

SAM.
>MY HANDS ARE STEADY.

KELLY. (*As* **CAROL ANN.**)
 TURN LEFT ONTO MAIN.
SAM.
 I BARELY EVEN HAVE TO STEER.
KELLY. (*As* **CAROL ANN.**)
 YOU SHOULD PROBABLY TRY STAYING IN ONE LANE.
SAM.
 AND I FEEL READY,
KELLY. (*As* **CAROL ANN.**)
 THIS PART SHOULD BE EASY.
SAM.
 THE ROAD IN FRONT OF ME IS CLEAR.
KELLY. (*As* **CAROL ANN.**)
 YOU'RE MAKING ME FEEL QUEASY, DEAR.
SAM.
 AND ALL AT ONCE I FEEL ALIVE.
KELLY. (*As* **CAROL ANN.**)
 ARE YOU READY FOR THE HIGHWAY?
SAM. Yes.
KELLY. (*As* **CAROL ANN.**)
 OK, THEN.
SAM & KELLY.
 DRIVE!

 DRIVE! **BEVERLY & ADAM.**
 DRIVE! OH
 AH
 DRIVE!

 (*Suddenly, the car lurches. The breaks squeal.
 The sound lives somewhere between a harsh
 reality and a nightmare.*)

 (**SAM** *doesn't look at* **KELLY.**)

KELLY. It is so awkward how that keeps happening!
SAM. (*Sarcastic.*) Maybe it's my cautious telling me not to
 go there.
KELLY. Or maybe / it's because you're ignoring –

SAM. *(Cutting her off, moving away from* **KELLY** *and the car.)* Let's give the statistician a quiz.

Mom! Over the course of a lifetime, please approximate the odds of striking it rich on *Antiques Roadshow*?

BEVERLY. *(Ready on a dime.)* 60,000 to 1.

SAM. The odds that a celebrity marriage will last a lifetime?

BEVERLY. Whose?

SAM. Uh, Sting?

BEVERLY. *(To audience.)* I love Sting. *(Back to business.)* 3 to 1.

SAM. The odds of becoming president?

BEVERLY. 10,000,000 to 1.

SAM. Struck by lightning?

BEVERLY. 580,000 to 1.

SAM. Fatally?

BEVERLY. 2,000,000 to 1.

> *(**KELLY** steps in.)*

KELLY. What are the odds of being hit by a car in the course of a year?

> *(**BEVERLY** looks at **KELLY** and then **SAM**, a little rattled.)*

BEVERLY. Ah… 18,000 to 1.

KELLY. And over the course of a lifetime?

BEVERLY. 228 to 1.

SAM. That will be all.

BEVERLY. You know the odds of *surviving* are a lot better than the odds of –

SAM. I know. That'll be all.

> *(**BEVERLY** doesn't have anything else to offer. She disappears into the shadows.)*

KELLY. Are you going to say it or am I?

SAM. I don't know what you're talking about.

KELLY. Fine. I'll do it.

> *(Savoring the big reveal.)*

I'm *dead.*

SAM. Kelly!

KELLY. What! The Band-Aid's ripped off. Now let's have the ceremony!

SAM. What ceremony?

KELLY. Uh, the one where you honor me?

SAM. You want a ceremony?

KELLY. I want a monument but I'll settle for a ceremony.

SAM. You're not dead yet. Not in the story.

KELLY. Oh this circus you're creating isn't avoidance? My bad.

SAM. Yeah, so I'd appreciate it if –

KELLY. *Honor me!*

["TOP TEN"]

SAM.

> WITH WHAT?

KELLY.

> THE TOP TEN WAYS FOR KELLY MANNING TO DIE.

SAM. No. Absolutely not.

KELLY. Come on! Top Ten. You love this game.

SAM. You're misappropriating it.

KELLY. *(Spoken in rhythm.)* You cannot stop this!

> NUMBER TEN.

I go skydiving without a parachute.

> NUMBER NINE.

SAM. Old age.

KELLY. Lame. Impossible.

> NUMBER EIGHT.
>
> ABDUCTED BY ALIENS WITH ENORMOUS GENITALIA.
>
> SEVEN.

> *(Beat.* **SAM***'s turn.* **KELLY** *will wait.)*

SAM. *(Reluctant.)* Kelly eats Mentos with Diet Coke and explodes.

KELLY.

> NOW THAT'S A DAMN FINE WAY
> FOR KELLY MANNING TO DIE. SIX!

SAM.

> SHE TOURS THE TUNDRA
> AND IS SWALLOWED BY A YETI.
> FIVE!

KELLY.

> I EAT SOME TOENAIL POLISH AT MY MANI-PEDI.
> FOUR!

SAM.

> HIT BY A METEOR.
> THREE!

KELLY.

> CAUGHT IN A GANG WAR.
> TWO!

SAM.

> KELLY LIKES CAFFEINE AND LOVES A RANDOM FLING
> SO ONE TIME AT A STARBUCKS
> SHE MAKES OUT WITH STING.
> AND STING IS ALL LIKE,
> "KELLY, I THINK YOU SHOULD COME ON TOUR."
> AND KELLY'S ALL LIKE,

KELLY.

> "I DON'T KNOW. IS THAT ARMANI? SURE!"
> But then Sting gets real clingy and when I say I have to
> go back to the states, he's like:

SAM. "I can't let you go."

KELLY. And I'm like, "Ew. You're my dad's age." And then, he
makes me listen to his *musical(?!)* and I'm like what's
with the ship? Why are you building the ship? But I
never find out because I'm literally bored to death.

SAM. It was scandalous.

KELLY.

> BUT NOT COMPARED TO
> THE NUMBER ONE WAY –

SAM.

> THE NUMBER ONE WAY –

KELLY. Hit by a car on the way home from the library!

SAM. Kelly!

KELLY. (*Rimshot.*) If only I'd never cracked a book. Too soon?

SAM. It's not funny.

KELLY. It kind of is... Funny-weird. Kelly Manning? In the library? With Professor Plum? More like the football coach. Did I say that out loud??

SAM. Shut up!

KELLY. Fine! Not ready to face your demons? Go ahead – sit in that memory swirl for a while.

["MEMORY JUMBLE"]

(*The memories bubble up.*)

ADAM.	**BEVERLY.**	
HEY SAM,	SLIDE THE CAR INTO GEAR,	
I WAS WONDERING	EASE YOUR FOOT OFF THE BRAKE.	
WOULD YOU BE MY DATE	THAT'S IT.	
		KELLY.
TO THE FRESHMAN FLING?	THAT'S ALL IT IS.	REMEMBER?
HEY, SAM.	NOW YOU LET IT GO.	REMEMBER?

(*A longish pause.*)

(**SAM** *is alone.*)

SAM. She was the sun. Or – no – a supernova. And I was in orbit around her. And what happens when the star – the supernova when it – when she –

KELLY. It's not about me, Sam.

SAM. Then what *is* it about?

> (**ADAM** *appears.*)

KELLY. Adam.

SAM. Seriously?

KELLY. No. Adam is here – just here –

> (**SAM** *looks around and sees* **ADAM**. *He waves.*)

ADAM. Hey. Just letting you know I'm – *around.*

KELLY. Just like real life! The Milwaukee to my Ibiza.

ADAM. You want to order a pizza?

KELLY. I rest my case. By the way, Adam is *not* going to help you move forward.

SAM. Kelly never liked Adam. She thought he was –

KELLY. Boring, an idiot, holding you back, tall?

SAM. But in some ways, he was actually maybe the most important part of my senior year –

KELLY. Is this about memory sex?

SAM. Kelly!

KELLY. It IS! Go get 'em, tiger!

> (**KELLY** *exits.*)

> (*The music shifts and we enter* **ADAM**'s *room. He fluffs a pillow on a truly dilapidated lawn chair.* **SAM** *watches him.*)

["SIMPLE AS THAT"]

SAM. Everyone I knew was trying to figure what their future would be. But after high school, Adam was taking over his dad's tire shop. It was all he wanted in the world. Well, that and me. No pressure.

ADAM. Hey – came up with a new slogan for the shop. "Everybody needs tires!" What do you think?

SAM. It's so – true.

ADAM. Thanks.

SAM. Being with Adam, hanging out in his room over his parents' garage – it was heaven.

ADAM. It wasn't a *room* so much as a *bachelor pad.*

SAM. Furnished with his childhood bed and a fetid lawn chair.

ADAM. That's not a word.

SAM. It's disgusting.

ADAM. I Febrezed it!

SAM.

ADAM LIKES TACOS AND PLAYING BOARD GAMES.

ADAM.

SAM KICKS MY ASS AT XBOX.

CALL IT WASTING TIME.

SAM.

CALL IT IMMATURE.

ADAM.

YOU'RE JUST JEALOUS 'CAUSE IT ROCKS.

SAM.

FOR SURE.

HE'S THE PERFECT GUY FOR A GIRL LIKE ME.

ADAM.

HOW MUCH PERFECTER COULD A GIRLFRIEND BE?

(**SAM** *viscerally feels his grammatical error. She smiles to cover.*)

SAM & ADAM.

PLAY A GAME, EAT SOME FOOD,

THEN MAKE OUT WHEN WE'RE IN THE MOOD.

SAM.

IT'S AS SIMPLE AS

PEAS IN A PEAPOD.

ADAM.

WE FIT LIKE LEGOS.

SAM & ADAM.

WE LIKE OUR CANDY DEEP-FRIED.

ADAM.

WE'RE LIKE BILL AND...

SAM.

TED.

ADAM.

> BEAVIS AND...

SAM.

> BUTTHEAD
> I'M THE BONNIE TO HIS...

> > *(Beat.)*

ADAM.

> WHO?

SAM.

> ...CLYDE

ADAM.

> SHE'S THE PERFECT GIRL FOR A GUY LIKE ME.

SAM.

> HOW MUCH *MORE* PERFECT COULD A BOYFRIEND BE?

ADAM & SAM.

> PLAY A GAME, EAT SOME FOOD,
> THEN MAKE OUT WHEN WE'RE IN THE MOOD.
> IT'S AS SIMPLE AS THAT.

SAM. So Adam didn't know the morphological rules for an adjective like perfect! Who cares? He *was* perfect. He is. It isn't his fault that I –

> *(A flash of **ADAM** waiting in the DMV, expectant. The fluorescent lights buzz.)*

That we –

> *(**ADAM** goes back to fixing up his room.)*

I don't know. Adam was everything I wanted. He's kind and fun and easy.

> IT'S AS SIMPLE AS...

ADAM. Tacos?

SAM. Tacos.

> *(**ADAM** heads off to find a phone and menu.)*

OK but *nothing* is as simple as tacos and Xbox. There's always something buried under the surface. A subtext – an unspoken desire.

(**ADAM** *returns with a menu.*)

ADAM. *(With relish, talking to the menu.)* Me gusto chorizo.

SAM. There was something Freudian in the way Adam talked about tacos.

ADAM. Yeah, baby, I'mma eat you *all* night.

SAM. Like he was sublimating all of his sexual frustration into food –

ADAM. Get in my mouth, you spicy barbacoa!

SAM. It was all too clear what Adam really wanted.

(*The lights shift.*)

["THE PROPOSAL"]

ADAM.

HAVE SEX WITH ME.
HAVE SEX WITH ME.
IN MY ROOM, I HAVE A PACK OF CONDOMS.
I HAVE SCENTED CANDLES AND I HAVE A BED.
HAVE SEX WITH ME,
THIS ONE'S AUTUMN POTPOURRI

JUST SLEEP WITH ME.

SAM.

WHAT SHOULD I DO?

ADAM.

PLEASE SLEEP WITH ME.

SAM.

SHOULD I HAVE SEX WITH YOU?

ADAM.

I WILL MAKE YOU PANCAKES IN THE MORNING.

BEVERLY.

PANCAKES ARE GOOD.

ADAM.

AND I'LL MAKE YOU
BREAKFAST IN BED;   **KELLY.**

WON'T YOU PLEASE HAVE   OH-OH-OH.
SEX WITH ME?
I MAKE GREAT DARJEELING TEA.

(Wind blows.)

HUNGER MAKES THE TIMID BOLD.

SAM.   **BEVERLY & KELLY.**

I CAN FEEL THE HUNGER.   AH

ADAM & SAM.

FEEL YOUR CARNAL   AH
URGES TAKING HOLD.

ADAM.

LEMME SAY SO I'M UNDERSTOOD:

ADAM, KELLY & BEVERLY.

SEX IS GOOD!

SAM.

SO GOOD!

ADAM.

EMBRACE YOUR DESTINY.*

SAM, KELLY & BEVERLY.

DESTINY –

ADAM.

OH BABY DON'T DENY MY HUNGRY PLEA.
HAVE SEX WITH ME.

SAM.

WHAT SHOULD I DO?

ADAM.

HAVE SEX WITH ME.

KELLY & BEVERLY.

HAVE SEX, OOH.

SAM.

SHOULD I HAVE SEX WITH YOU?

KELLY & BEVERLY.

HAVE SEX.

ADAM.

MAYBE NOT TODAY
MAYBE TOMORROW.

KELLY & BEVERLY.

HAVE SEX TOMORROW.

---

*After this point, the song can be cut off abruptly at any time by Kelly yelling "Nooooooooo!" thereby frustrating applause / button.

ADAM.
MAYBE NOT TOMORROW
ALL.
MAYBE IN A WEEK. HAVE SEX –
ADAM.
WITH ME,
AND YOUR DINNER WILL BE FREE!
KELLY & BEVERLY.
HAVE SEX WITH ME.

ADAM.	**SAM, KELLY & BEVERLY**.
HAVE SEX WITH ME!	AH

KELLY. Nooooooooooooo – this is the weirdest orgy ever!! No wonder you're a virgin!

SAM. Oh, come on! He can't really be talking about tacos!

KELLY. Have you *met* Adam?

BEVERLY. You know, in the wild, the male performs for the *female*. He puffs up his plumage and the female decides: is he worthy?

KELLY. Is he, Sam? And while we're here, Adam – can you define the word "carnal"?

ADAM. Huh?

SAM. Fine! OK? The actual conversation went a lot more like this:

(Scene reset. **BEVERLY** *and* **KELLY** *disappear.)*

ADAM. So – what do you want?

SAM. What do you mean what do *I* want?

ADAM. For dinner?

SAM. Why don't you just come out and say what *you* really want?

ADAM. I want tacos.

SAM. You want sex.

ADAM. I said tacos but...do you want –

SAM. See?

ADAM. What?

SAM. That's all it's ever about with you!

ADAM. Is this something where you, like, want pizza and I said the wrong kind of food and –

SAM. Oh, I'm totally satisfied and I don't need anything else.

ADAM. So you're *not* hungry.

SAM. Not everyone has an insatiable appetite, Adam! Some people can actually go, like, two minutes without thinking about satisfying some base carnal need!

ADAM. *(Tentative.)* Is it, like, that time of the month?

SAM. No, Adam. I'm not having my *period*.

ADAM. Jesus! You don't have to say it.

SAM. It's just a word.

ADAM. Yeah. But it's an idea too.

> *(Beat.)*

SAM. *(A realization.)* You're really talking about tacos.

ADAM. We can eat whatever you want.

SAM. I'm an idiot.

ADAM. I'm just, like, hungry.

SAM. Yeah.

ADAM. So I'm gonna go order, OK?

> *(He kisses her carefully.)*

And then we're gonna get *down* –

SAM. What?

ADAM. On tacos.

["SEX ON THE BRAIN"]

> *(He's teasing her. She pushes him. He pushes her back. They kiss. It's real and lovely. Then he leaves. She watches him go: nostalgia personified.)*

SAM. *(To us.)* I had sex on the brain. *I* did. But how do you talk about that? How do you come out and say what you want? It wasn't just – sex. It was everything. I never said what I wanted, except – except with Kelly. Except – there was that one night.

["THERE WAS A PARTY"]

KELLY. *(In flashback, teasing.)*
> WHAT –
> YOU THINK IT'S GONNA BITE?

>> *(A memory flashes. A distant phone ring. The memory morphs and is replaced by another. A club beat pulses.)*

SAM. A starry sky. A club beat. We were visiting the one school we'd both gotten into. Where was Kelly? The beat got louder. I was pushing through crowds in a stairwell of this dorm or frat. Everyone was yelling. I didn't stop to memorize the details. I didn't know how much the night would matter. I opened a door.
> THERE WAS A PARTY,
> A DJ, A BEAT PULSED ON.
> A COLLEGE, A CAMPUS.
> A MANICURED LAWN.
> I WAITED FOR KELLY 'CAUSE SHE WAS MY RIDE.
> I HAD COMBED THE WHOLE DANCE FLOOR
> AND WANDERED OUTSIDE
> THE PARTY...
> OR HALLWAY...
> AND IT WAS –
> AND IT WAS APRIL AND CHILLY
> OR LATE MARCH AND WARM.
> OUR TOUR GUIDE AND KELLY WERE BACK AT HIS DORM.
> THE WHOLE SKY WAS SPINNING.
> I MIGHT HAVE BEEN DRUNK.
> AS I STEADIED MYSELF ON THE ROOF OF HER TRUNK
> ALL ALONE, WAS I LOST OR WAS I ALIVE?
> IN THE SPACE, IN THE HOLE SHE CREATED.
> NO ANCHOR.
> ABANDONED.
> I WAITED.

>> *(The light sound of crickets chirping).*

>> (**KELLY**, *drunk, runs on stage.*)

KELLY. Sam! I thought you were lost forever! You will never believe this.

(*She hands* SAM *a flask.*)

SAM. You got laid?

(SAM *smells it and drinks.*)

KELLY. I mean – yes? But this is so much more important. Did you know that there's a class here *called* "Sex"?

SAM. I doubt it's about mating rituals.

KELLY. Mmm. The TA would have me believe otherwise.

SAM. That idiot was a TA?

KELLY. Oh, the tour guide? I dropped him hours ago. We DFMO'd* for a while and then the *TA* was at the party...

SAM. DFMO'd?

KELLY. Dance floor make out. It's a thing.

SAM. Way to man-hop.

KELLY. Way to slut-shame. Someday, you too will hit a point where a guy is like, "Let me save you, let me take care of you, let me – like – build you a house, and we'll have babies," and that's when you bolt. Even if you're mid-orgasm.

SAM. Whatever.

KELLY. Wow. I kind of hate you right now. This is our first – maybe *only* – night of college together and you are actually the worst.

SAM. Come on – I mean. You can't like this place. Some dude streaked the physics class.

KELLY. That is literally the only way I like physics.

SAM. The whole college machine is a cliché.

KELLY. So is your angst.

SAM. Wait – are you actually going to go here?

KELLY. Where else am I going to go?

SAM. (*Overly passionate, a little drunk.*) Paris? Guatemala? California – you don't have to conform to some metric

---

*Pronounced "dee-eff-moed"

of success. You have a car. You have gumption and, and, and drive and – I don't know – Kelly Manning doesn't just *do* what everyone else does. She doesn't follow the same rules. She's otherworldly. She's one of the mad ones.

KELLY. You're drunk.

SAM. I'm not drunk.

KELLY. I like it.

SAM. I'm not drunk.

KELLY. OK, drunky. Let's do it.

SAM. What.

KELLY. Let's go.

SAM. What? Where?

KELLY. Who cares? Let's go be mad like in that book. Like, like burning like candles. Like Jerouac.

SAM. Jack Kerouac?

KELLY. That's what I said. Tell me the part about the candles.

SAM. Uh.

KELLY. Do not pretend you don't have it memorized.

> (**SAM** *gives* **KELLY** *a look.* **KELLY** *returns it.* **SAM** *concedes.*)
>
> (*Time stretches.*)

SAM. He said, "The only ones for me are the mad ones –"

["THE MAD ONES"]

> (*A guitar groove begins.*)

"Mad to talk, mad to be saved, desirous of everything at the same time –"

KELLY.

IF WE'RE GONNA GO, WE GOTTA GO TONIGHT.

SAM. "The ones who never yawn or say a commonplace thing but burn, burn, burn like fabulous yellow roman candles exploding like spiders across the stars..."

KELLY.

OH, IF WE'RE GONNA GO, WE GOTTA GO TONIGHT.
GO TONIGHT.
GO TONIGHT.
I'M IN.

SAM.

FOR WHAT?

KELLY.

WE'RE TAKING THE RISK.
WE'RE THE FOOLS WHO WILL NEVER LEARN.
PUSHED TO THE EDGE.
OUT ON THE LEDGE
WILL YOU DIE OUT OR BURN, BURN, BURN?

DON'T ASK IF YOU CAN.
NO, THAT'S THE MISTAKE GIRLS MAKE.
'CAUSE THOSE GOOD OLD BOYS
THEY HAD THEIR GOOD OLD DAYS
BUT NOW THEY'RE GONE
AND NOW THEIR WORLD IS OURS TO TAKE.

WE'RE MAD TO GO,
MAD TO DRIVE,
MAD TO BE ALIVE.
WE'RE CHASING STARS –
A THOUSAND SUNS.
THE MAD, MAD ONES
OH WHOA OH OH OH

SAM.

OH WHOA OH OH OH.

KELLY.

OH WHOA OH OH OH.

SAM.

OH WHOA OH OH OH.

KELLY.

WE BREAK THE LOCK,
WE KICK THE DOOR,
MAD

SAM.

>MAD

KELLY & SAM.

>TO REACH FOR MORE.

KELLY.

>WE MAKE THE RULES,
>WE MAKE A VOW
>TO BE MAD,

SAM.

>MAD.

KELLY.

>GIRL, WE'RE WHAT MATTER NOW.
>
>OK. First thing's first. You have to go tell that TA I'm not coming back.

SAM. What?

KELLY.

>IF WE'RE GONNA GO, WE GOTTA GO TONIGHT,
>Screw it. He'll figure it out.
>
>IF WE'RE GONNA GO, WE GOTTA GO TONIGHT,
>Where are my keys?

SAM. Just calm down. There's planning involved. What are we living on? Who's paying our cell phone bills?

KELLY. Well A:

>(**KELLY** *smashes* **SAM**'s *phone.*)

SAM. Kelly!

KELLY. And two, Sam:

>IF WE'RE GONNA GO, WE GOTTA GO TONIGHT,
>GO TONIGHT, GO TONIGHT.

SAM.

>YOU'RE DRUNK.

KELLY.

>*YOU'RE DRUNK!*
>IF WE'RE GONNA GO, WE GOTTA GO TONIGHT,
>GO TONIGHT, GO TONIGHT.

SAM. I *am* drunk! And I only have a permit. We can't –

KELLY. STOP SAYING CAN'T!!

SAM. STOP TELLING ME WHAT TO DO!!!

KELLY.

IF WE'RE GONNA GO, WE GOTTA GO TONIGHT,
IF WE'RE GONNA GO, WE GOTTA GO TONIGHT

SAM.

IF WE'RE GONNA GO, WE GOTTA GO TONIGHT –

KELLY & SAM.

GO TONIGHT, GO TONIGHT!

SAM.

WITHOUT ANY PLAN,
JUST THE KEYS AND A RADIO.

KELLY.

YEAH.

SAM & KELLY.

LIVING FOR US.
KICKING UP DUST.

SAM.

WE JUST PICK UP AND GO, GO, GO.

KELLY.

YES!

SAM.

IT'S NEVER OR NOW.

KELLY.

NEVER OR NOW, YES!

SAM & KELLY.

TIME TO TAKE YOUR FOOT OFF THE BRAKE.

SAM.

YEAH, THOSE GOOD OLD BOYS
THEY HAD THEIR GOOD OLD DAYS

KELLY & SAM.

BUT NOW THEY'RE GONE

SAM.

AND NOW THEIR WORLD

KELLY.

IS OURS TO TAKE.

SAM.

IS OURS TO TAKE.

SAM & KELLY.

WE'RE MAD TO GO,
MAD TO DRIVE,

SAM.

MAD

KELLY.

MAD

SAM & KELLY.

TO BE ALIVE.
WE'RE CHASING STARS,
A THOUSAND SUNS.

SAM.

THE MAD

KELLY.

MAD

SAM & KELLY.

MAD ONES.

KELLY.

OH WHOA OH OH OH.

SAM.

OH WHOA OH OH OH.

KELLY.

OH WHOA OH OH OH.

SAM.

OH WHOA OH OH OH.

KELLY.

IF WE'RE GONNA GO WE GOTTA GO TONIGHT,
GO TONIGHT, GO TONIGHT.

IF WE'RE GONNA GO WE GOTTA GO TONIGHT,
GO TONIGHT.

(The memory begins to dissolve.)

SAM.

BUT WE DIDN'T GO,
DIDN'T GO, DIDN'T GO

GO THAT NIGHT,
DID WE?

  (A beat. Are we going here?)

KELLY.

NO WE DIDN'T GO,
DIDN'T GO, DIDN'T GO
GO THAT NIGHT.

SAM. *(To us.)*

I MEAN OBVIOUSLY.
THE WHOLE THING WENT SOUTH.
PER USUAL, KELLY'S ONLY PLAN
WAS RUNNING HER MOUTH.

KELLY.

OH, BUT WHO LET DOWN WHO?

SAM.

WHO LET DOWN WHO?

KELLY.

WHO LET DOWN WHO?

SAM.

WHO LET DOWN WHO?

KELLY.

YOU WERE THE ONE WHO PUT ON THE BRAKES.

SAM.

I WANTED TO GRADUATE FIRST.

KELLY.

YOU DIDN'T HAVE WHAT IT TAKES.

SAM.

OH, WHO LET DOWN WHO?

KELLY.

WHO LET DOWN WHO?

SAM.

LIKE YOU EVER FOLLOWED THROUGH
ON A SINGLE WORD YOU SAID.

KELLY.

IF WE'D ONLY GONE THAT NIGHT
THEN I WOULDN'T BE DEAD.

SAM & KELLY.

TELL ME –

SAM.

WHO LET DOWN WHO?

KELLY.

WHO LET DOWN WHO?

SAM.

WHO LET DOWN WHO?

KELLY.

WHO LET DOWN WHO?

SAM.

YOU!

KELLY.

YOU!

SAM.

YOU!

KELLY & SAM.

YOU!

YOU!

YOU!

YOU!

(They reach an impasse. The music continues. They're not speaking to each other.)

*(After a moment, **KELLY** does a little dance move. **SAM** half-heartedly responds. Then **SAM** does another. **KELLY** responds.)*

(Then they start going back and forth. It's kind of stupid but also kind of funny to them – maybe only to them. It's weird and private.)

KELLY.

OH WHOA OH OH OH

SAM.

OH WHOA OH OH OH

(Dance break.)

KELLY & SAM.

KELLY.	**SAM.**
OH	OH
MAD	MAD
TO GO MAD	
TO DRIVE	
MAD	

SAM.

MAD

KELLY & SAM.

TO BE ALIVE
WE'RE CHASING STARS –
A THOUSAND SUNS.

SAM.

THE MAD

KELLY.

MAD

KELLY & SAM.

MAD ONES.

SAM.

OH WHOA OH OH OH.

KELLY.

OH WHOA OH OH OH.

SAM.

OH WHOA OH OH OH.

KELLY.

OH WHOA OH OH OH.

KELLY & SAM.

WE BREAK THE LOCK.
WE KICK THE DOOR.

SAM.

MAD

KELLY.

MAD

KELLY & SAM.

TO REACH FOR MORE

WE MAKE THE RULES,
WE MAKE A VOW
TO BE MAD
GIRL, WE'RE WHAT MATTER NOW

SAM.

OH WHOA OH OH OH

(She turns to **KELLY** *to echo her and* **KELLY***'s gone. The song ends abruptly.)*

III.

*(**SAM**'s back where she started. Still in a daydream. Car, keys, no movement forward.)*

(Disorienting. Awkward.)

SAM. Oh.

(She looks around.)

(The ominous sound of a low synth drone.)

Um.

The sun – I meant to say –

I meant to say the sun doesn't make a black hole. When it – the sun is over 100 times bigger than the earth. The earth's – poof – a piece of dust. Infinitesimal. Inconsequential. The sun even – poof. But supernovas. They're 10 times. 20 times bigger...

There's this –. This –.

["THE SUN"]

You get sucked in.

Time stops. No light.

Black.

*(A beat. **SAM** gets lost.)*

She was...

She was –

(She shakes it off.)

By the end of that weekend, I had let Kelly believe I was going to state school with her. My mom thought I was going to *her* Ivy alma mater. I was literally hiding my stash under my bed.

Where most kids have pot, I had a deposit for Harvard. My guidance counselor called an emergency session with my mom.

*(**SAM** joins her **MOM** and **ADAM** in a grim scene, waiting for the **GUIDANCE COUNSELOR**.)*

BEVERLY. Why don't you explain why Adam was there?

SAM. The session was on the day I broke my mom's car.

BEVERLY. Crashed.

ADAM. I drove Sam and her mom from my auto body shop to the meeting.

BEVERLY. And stayed.

>   (**ADAM** *grins.*)

SAM. The guidance counselor was late, as usual.

>   (*Beat.*)

> Ahem. The guidance counselor? Kelly.

>   (**KELLY** *appears.*)

KELLY. What?

SAM. The guidance counselor. Can you – [play the role...]

KELLY. Seriously? I have to do everything around here! Hold on.

>   (*All of* **KELLY**'s *reluctance vanishes as she prepares for the role of their uber-positive and semi-psychic* **GUIDANCE COUNSELOR**, *complete with pashmina.*)

> (*As* **GUIDANCE COUNSELOR**.) Wow! Finally! I get to meet the proud mama bear of our third *female* valedictorian. She is "wow"! Right?

> (*To* **ADAM**.) And you are?

ADAM. Adam. I'm a student here.

KELLY. (*As* **GUIDANCE COUNSELOR**, *so understanding.*) Oh! Did you drop out?

ADAM. No.

KELLY. (*As* **GUIDANCE COUNSELOR**.) Mm.

>   (*Pivoting.*)

> Well, Samantha! What's on the vision board for next year?

BEVERLY. Samantha is going to Harvard.

KELLY. (*As* **GUIDANCE COUNSELOR**.) Samantha,

["GUIDANCE COUNSELOR"]

look at you! Your options are limitless! Sure, you can fulfill your overbearing mother's dream or you could create your *own* destiny at – say – a state school with co-ed frats!

BEVERLY. The girl got into three Ivys. She's *going* to an Ivy.

KELLY. *(As* **GUIDANCE COUNSELOR,** *all smiles.)* Some people think Ivys are overrated. What does Samantha think?

SAM. Um – I... I don't... I really –

KELLY. *(As* **GUIDANCE COUNSELOR.***)* Let's all say something we *want*. Why don't you start us off, Bev?

BEVERLY. I want the best possible future for my daughter.

KELLY. *(As* **GUIDANCE COUNSELOR.***)* Uh-huh and –

(Ready to move on to the next person.)

BEVERLY. I want you to call me Beverly.

KELLY. *(As* **GUIDANCE COUNSELOR.***)* Oh!

BEVERLY. And I want my car fixed.

KELLY. *(As* **GUIDANCE COUNSELOR.***)* Oh –

(Done? She's done.)

'kay. Good. Good. *(To* **ADAM.***)* And what did you say your name was?

ADAM. Adam. You're *my* guidance counselor.

KELLY. *(As* **GUIDANCE COUNSELOR.***)* OK. If that's what you want! And what does *Samantha* want?

(A clock ticks in the distance.)

SAM. *(To us.)* Isn't it weird how certain kinds of women are allergic to each other? Like don't we all want the same things – respect, equal pay, the end of the *Bachelor* franchise? But there's a line in the sand and you have to choose which side you're on. I want...

(The clock ticks again.)

KELLY. *(As* **GUIDANCE COUNSELOR.***)* Yes?

(Everyone leans in.)

SAM. I want to, uh…go to an Ivy.

    (**BEVERLY** *suddenly dons college paraphernalia.*)

BEVERLY.
    FIGHT FIERCELY, HARVARD!
    FIGHT, FIGHT, FIGHT!

KELLY. *(Real* **KELLY**, *not hiding her disdain.)* Really.

SAM. Yeah. An Ivy League education is right for me.

    (**KELLY** *throws off her costume, annoyed with*
    SAM *for not standing up to her mother, not*
    telling what **KELLY** *thought was the truth.)*

(To audience.) I'd already broken her car that day.
I couldn't shatter her life-long dream of having a legacy
child.

BEVERLY. *(At* **KELLY**.*)* In your face!

    (**BEVERLY** *tries to high five* **SAM**.*)*

SAM. My mom is an intense woman. Professionally, she
makes college freshmen cry. When I was little, at
Halloween, she dressed me up as Eleanor Roosevelt for
three years straight. She's not a *mom* mom.

BEVERLY. Samantha, do you remember when we used to do
Girl Scouts?

SAM. Mom, we didn't do Girl Scouts.

    (**SAM** *starts to exit.)*

BEVERLY. But don't you wish we did?

["I KNOW MY GIRL"]

    (**BEVERLY** *turns her intense gaze on us.)*

BEVERLY.
    EIGHTEEN YEARS HAVE COME AND GONE.
    I RAISED MY DAUGHTER WELL.
    EIGHTEEN YEARS SHE'S MY WHOLE LIFE,
    AND NOW IT GOES TO HELL.
    I KNOW MY GIRL AND I KNOW HER EYES.
    AND SHE NEVER RUNS AND SHE NEVER LIES.
    THERE'S SOMETHING WRONG,

IT'S PLAIN TO SEE.
'CAUSE HER HEAD'S A MESS
AND HER HEART'S A WHIRL.
I KNOW THOSE EYES.
I KNOW MY GIRL.
AND SHE'S GONNA TALK TO ME.

> (**SAM** *and* **ADAM** *enter and sit at the kitchen table.*)

> (**BEVERLY** *enters in an apron, bearing a plate of freshly baked cookies.*)

BEVERLY.

I MADE COOKIES.
HAVE A COOKIE.

SAM. I have a test to study for.

> (**SAM** *exits.* **BEVERLY** *zeroes in on* **ADAM.***)*

BEVERLY.

I MADE COOKIES.

ADAM.

I LIKE COOKIES.

BEVERLY.

HAVE A COOKIE, HAVE A FEW.
AND THEN YOU'LL SIT AND TALK –
WE'LL SIT AND TALK.
YOU'LL TELL ME
WHO SHE'S HANGING OUT WITH,
AND WHO SHE'S IN A FIGHT WITH,
AND WHY SHE ISN'T TELLING ME?
HAS SHE STARTED HUFFING,
OR DID YOU GET HER PREGNANT,
OR IS SHE HIGH ON LSD?

> (*Beat.*)

SAM. (*Offstage.*) Adam!

ADAM. I dunno. Maybe she's having her...y'know.

> (*He grabs a cookie. He runs.*)

BEVERLY.
> I WON'T BE DISCOURAGED.
> I REFUSE TO BE OUTDONE.
> THE GAME IS FAR FROM OVER.
> HELL, IT'S ONLY JUST BEGUN.
> I KNOW MY GIRL AND I KNOW HER EYES,
> AND SHE NEVER RUNS AND SHE NEVER LIES.
> I KNOW SHE'S DYIN' TO LET ME IN.
> BUT HER HEAD'S A MESS
> AND HER HEART'S A WHIRL.
> I KNOW THOSE EYES,
> I KNOW MY GIRL.
> SO LET THE GAME BEGIN.

> > (**BEVERLY** *and* **SAM** *are out shopping together.*)

> DO YOU NEED TO GO INTO THE CVS FOR SOMETHING?

SAM. No. Why?

BEVERLY.
> YOU MIGHT NEED TO GO INTO THE CVS FOR SOMETHING?

> > (*Beat.*)

SAM. Do you *think* I need to go into CVS?

BEVERLY.
> *AND* IF YOU NEED TO GO INTO THE CVS
> FOR SOMETHING,
> I COULD COME ALONG.
> I'LL HELP YOU *BUY* THE SOMETHING...
> TEACH YOU TO *USE* THE SOMETHING...
> DO YOU NEED TO GO INTO THE CVS FOR SOMETHING?
> ANYTHING...
> HELP. ME.

> > (**BEVERLY** *exits.* **ADAM** *and* **KELLY** *appear.*)

SAM. She's trying to kill me. Is she trying to kill me?

> > (*They stare at her.*)

ADAM. I dunno, maybe she's having her –

KELLY. Period period period period period!

> > (**BEVERLY** *enters grandly in a disheveled apron.*)

BEVERLY. *(Aggressive.)*
    I MADE COOKIES.
KELLY. Oh! Nice.
BEVERLY.
    HAVE A COOKIE.
ADAM. Dude – it's a trap.

       *(**ADAM** runs off.)*

BEVERLY.
    JUST ONE COOKIE.
    Oh wait!

       (She hurls the cookies away.)

       *(She shows **SAM** an empty plate.)*

    NO MORE COOKIES.
    YOU WAITED TOO LONG.
    NOW THE COOKIES ARE GONE.
    SAM, YOU HAVE TO EAT COOKIES
    WHILE I'M STILL ALIVE
    TO MAKE YOU COOKIES.
    MY MOTHER MADE ME COOKIES.
    WE WOULD TALK THROUGH THE NIGHT.
    SHE MADE EV'RYTHING RIGHT.
    I'M SO HAPPY I ATE COOKIES
    WITH MY DEVOTED MOTHER, MY GUIDE.
    BEFORE SHE DIED.

       (Beat.)

SAM. I was trapped.
KELLY. *(Settling in for a show.)* She was trapped.
SAM. *(To **BEVERLY**.)* OK. Fine. Don't freak out.
BEVERLY. When have I ever –
KELLY. *(Mouth full of cookie.)* Puh-lease.

      *(**BEVERLY** glares at **KELLY**.)*

    These cookies are great, Bev.

      (She takes another.)

BEVERLY. *(To* **SAM,** *taking so many high roads.)* I won't freak out.

SAM. All right. There is one thing.

KELLY. Oh my God. You had secret sex with Adam and you're pregnant!

BEVERLY. I knew it!

SAM. What?

BEVERLY. Oh honey, honey. I'm so glad you came to me. We will figure this out.

SAM. No! I am 100% not even *possibly* pregnant. At all. I just – I don't want to go to college.

(*Beat.*)

BEVERLY. What?

KELLY. I don't understand.

SAM. I've been thinking about it a lot and I think I need to take some time, figure things out for myself, maybe drive –

KELLY. Wait – I thought you were coming to college with *me.*

BEVERLY. No. We sent a deposit to Harvard.

SAM. Not *technically.*

BEVERLY. Excuse me?

SAM. Listen –

KELLY. Sam sent a deposit to my school. Tell her.

SAM. I – no. I didn't. I –

KELLY. You lied to me?

SAM. No – I just –

BEVERLY. You see that? Sam might talk a big game about frats and keg parties but when push comes to shove, she's going to make the smart choice –

SAM. That's not –

KELLY. Because my school isn't "smart" enough for her?

BEVERLY. Frankly, no, it isn't.

SAM. Mom!

BEVERLY. She's a C student and you're the valedictorian.

KELLY. You don't know my grades.

BEVERLY. I know you're the source of all of Sam's bad ideas.

KELLY. You're blaming *me* for Sam's bad ideas? What about Adam? What about you?

SAM. Enough.

KELLY. You've got her wound up so tight I'm surprised she's not teetering on a ledge somewhere.

SAM. Kelly, get out.

KELLY. With pleasure.

>*(She turns back to* **BEVERLY.**)*

I am a solid B student but I'll deny I ever told you that.

>*(***KELLY*** leaves.)*

>*(Beat.)*

BEVERLY. 20 to 1.

SAM. What's that?

BEVERLY. The odds you get into an Ivy.

SAM. I'm not saying I'll never go to college.

BEVERLY. Then what do you want to do?

SAM. I don't know. I –

BEVERLY. That's not an answer.

SAM. I want to not know for once. I want something I can't see coming. Anything.

BEVERLY. This is about that damn book.

SAM. It's not about a –

BEVERLY. You don't even have a license. You are not going to go out on a road trip alone to make some kind of point.

SAM. It's not about making a point.

BEVERLY. Girls get one shot, Sam.

["MILES TO GO"]

Girls don't get to fail.

A LONE BOY ON THE HIGHWAY,

A FUTURE UNDEFINED,
THE REBEL SOUL THAT GOT AWAY
AND LEFT HIS PAST BEHIND.

A LONE BOY ON THE HIGHWAY,
YOU'VE SEEN HIS FACE BEFORE.
TWO PATHS DIVERGED AND YOU WENT RIGHT
BUT HE'S LEFT WANTING MORE.
AND WHERE HE'LL LAND,
THIS TOWN WILL NEVER KNOW –
HE'S GOT MILES AND MILES AND MILES TO GO.

HIS SHOES THAT POUND THE PAVEMENT,
THE DAYDREAM HE CAN'T NAME.
NOW MAKE THAT BOY A LONELY GIRL
AND TELL ME SHE'S THE SAME.
THE BOY YOU CALL A REBEL,
THE GIRL – SHE'S RUNNING SCARED,
'CAUSE ANY GIRL WHO'S ON HER OWN
IS OUT THERE UNPREPARED.
SHE LOOKS AWAY.
SHE KEEPS HER PROFILE LOW.
SHE'S GOT MILES AND MILES AND MILES TO GO.

THE GAME HAS BEEN RIGGED
BUT I LEARNED TO PLAY.
AND I'M NOT THE ENEMY.
I PAVED THE WAY.
I STOOD IN MY OWN MOTHER'S KITCHEN –

    (Lights begin to transition.)

THE DOOR SLAMMED BEHIND ME.
I BLINK AND I'M YOU AGAIN –

    *(1982. **BEVERLY** is driving down the highway,*
    windows down, wind in her hair.)

BEVERLY.

I'M SINGING JANIS JOPLIN
AT THE TOP OF MY LUNGS.
I'M CURSING LIKE A SAILOR
AND I'M SPEAKING IN TONGUES.
FREEDOM

FREEDOM
FREEDOM.

(**BEVERLY** *returns to the present moment.*)

SAM. It's different now.

BEVERLY. Some things are. *This* isn't.

A LONE BOY ON THE HIGHWAY.
YOU THINK "THAT COULD BE ME"
BUT YOU WERE BORN A WOMAN AND
YOU'LL NEVER BE THAT FREE.
THE GLASS CRACKS IN THE CEILING
AND WOMEN SWELL WITH PRIDE.
BUT WHEN A WOMAN BREAKS THE RULES
THE WORLD'S NOT ON HER SIDE.
THE WHEELS OF CHANGE –
THEY MOVE SO GODDAMN SLOW.

YES, WE'VE COME MILES AND MILES AND MILES,
BUT WE'VE GOT MILES AND MILES
AND MILES
AND MILES AND MILES AND MILES
AND MILES
TO GO.

(*The moment shifts.* **BEVERLY** *disappears.*)

(**SAM** *sees* **KELLY** *in another area of the stage at an ancient library payphone.* **SAM** *walks toward* **KELLY**, *an observer.*)

KELLY. (*Into the phone.*) See? It's your fault. You never pick up. Whatever, I don't care if you go to my college, Sam. I didn't think you would – it's not, like, – your kind of – I get it. I'm not mad about that. I am mad though. Like, 'cause you didn't pick up, and 'cause you say I don't call you. And obviously I do. So. Stop saying that. Anyway, I hope you're doing something worthwhile. Like – sealing the deal with Milwaukee? 'Cause you know what I say – what, you think it's gonna bite?

(*Suddenly,* **SAM** *is in* **ADAM**'s *room.*)

ADAM. Sam?

SAM. I want to have sex.

ADAM. What?

SAM. Now. I want to have sex now. Strip!

ADAM. *(To us.)* Can I just... Three years.

SAM. Shh. Don't talk. Take your pants off.

> *(**SAM** starts to undress him. **ADAM** is tempted, then conflicted.)*

ADAM. *(Finally.)* No – no. There is something messed up here.

SAM. What, something has to be wrong for me to want to –

> *(Barely able to say it.)*

– make love to you?

ADAM. Yep. Yes. That is exactly what I'm saying.

SAM. And *I'm* saying I wanna *do it.*

ADAM. Shut up. Put your pants on.

> *(He waits for this to happen. **SAM** begrudgingly puts her pants back on.)*

OK. What's going on?

SAM. Nothing. I told my mom I didn't want to go to college. And Kelly was there and they both flipped out and –

ADAM. You don't want to go to college?

SAM. No, OK? Why is that such a trigger? I mean – my mom literally gave me, like, a treatise on the limitations of womanhood to guilt me into going. So I don't need to hear it from you too.

ADAM. I think you should do what you want to do.

SAM. You do?

ADAM. Yeah. Even if you don't know what it is yet – you're smart. You'll figure it out.

> *(**SAM** kisses **ADAM.**)*

["SAY THE WORD"]

SAM. How do you do that?

ADAM. What?

SAM. Somehow you've never put any pressure on me. About anything.

ADAM. I just want you to be happy.

SAM. I am. I'm happy here.

ADAM. Good. Me too.

SAM. Maybe I do know what I want.

> SOMETIMES WHEN I LOOK AT YOU
> I DON'T KNOW WHY YOU WAIT.
> SCHOOL GIRL IN A LITTLE WORLD
> WHO LEARNS EV'RYTHING LATE.
> I'VE ALWAYS HAD ALL THE ANSWERS
> NOW I DON'T HAVE A CLUE.
>
> SOME NIGHTS WHEN THE CLOUDS ARE THICK
> AND THE WIND STARTS TO BLOW.
> I STARE OUT THE WINDOW
> WOND'RING WHERE I WILL GO.
> I TURN THE LIGHT OUT,
> UNDER THE COVERS ALL I THINK OF IS YOU.
> JUST YOU.
>
> SAY THE WORD,
> AND I JUST MIGHT LISTEN.
> SAY THE WORD,
> AND YOU MIGHT GET YOUR WAY.
> LET ME GO IF IT'S EASIER,
> BUT SAY THE WORD,
> AND I MIGHT HAVE TO STAY.

ADAM. Don't screw around with me, Sam.

SAM. I'm not. I'm figuring out what I want.

ADAM. What's that?

SAM. You.

> MEANWHILE THERE'S SO MANY THINGS
> THAT WE DON'T UNDERSTAND.
> I DON'T KNOW WHY I TREMBLE
> WHEN YOU REACH FOR MY HAND.
> I DIDN'T KNOW HOW TO LOVE
> UNTIL YOU SWEPT ME AWAY.

SO SAY THE WORD,
AND I JUST MIGHT LISTEN.
SAY THE WORD,
AND YOU MIGHT GET YOUR WAY.
LET ME GO IF IT'S EASIER,
BUT SAY THE WORD,
AND I MIGHT HAVE TO STAY.

I WANNA LOVE.
I WANNA RIDE.
I WANNA BE THE GIRL THERE BY YOUR SIDE.
JUST TELL ME WHEN.
JUST TELL ME HOW.
TELL ME, I'M READY NOW,
TODAY!
SAY THE WORD,

ADAM.

SAY THE WORD.

SAM.

AND I JUST MIGHT LISTEN. **ADAM.**

SAY THE WORD,   SAY THE WORD AND I
AND YOU MIGHT
GET YOUR WAY   WHATEVER YOU SAY
LET ME GO
IF IT'S EASIER, BUT

ADAM & SAM.

SAY THE WORD.

SAM.

AND I MIGHT HAVE TO STAY.

(**SAM** *and* **ADAM** *move toward the bed as the lights dim.*)

IV.

["IN MY DREAM"]

(When the lights come back up, **ADAM** *is sleeping and* **SAM** *is sitting on the edge of the bed.)*

That night, after we had sex for the first time, I dreamed about Kelly. I'd like to say I sensed the phone call I was about to get but it was probably because of the fight we'd just had. Anyway – there she was in my dream – pulling me out of Adam's bed.

KELLY. We have got to get out of here.

SAM. Kelly?

KELLY. Let's go, Sam. Up and –

(Seeing **ADAM**.*)*

Adam – this isn't your room. Wait. Samantha Brown. You had sexual intercourse.

SAM. I –

KELLY. Was it everything you ever wanted?

SAM. I don't know. It was sweet.

KELLY. Give it time. Come on, get your stuff and let's go.

SAM. I can't – I had that fight with my mom –

KELLY. Call her from the road.

SAM. Why don't you stay here?

KELLY. At Adam's house? It smells like socks.

SAM. No. Kelly, can't we just go to my house, and eat popcorn and watch movies? Why do we always have to go somewhere? Why can't we –

*(***SAM***'s cell phone rings.)*

(It rings again.)

["MOVING ON"]

KELLY. Aren't you going to get that?

     (Ring.)

Sam?

     (Ring.)

KELLY. Don't you think you should wake up and answer the phone?

     (Beat. Lightbulb.)

SAM. No.

     (Ring.)

KELLY. Sam. You have to.

SAM.

    WHAT IF I *DON'T*?

     (Ring.)

KELLY. What do you mean what if you don't?

SAM.

    WHAT IF I *DON'T*?

KELLY. You did!

     (Ring.)

SAM.

    BUT IF I DON'T PICK UP THE PHONE,
    IT'S SORT OF LIKE IT NEVER HAPPENED.

     (She waits for **KELLY** *to catch her drift.)*

KELLY. What are you *talking* about?

SAM.

    LIKE THE *PHONE CALL…*

     (Ring.)

    NEVER HAPPENED,
    AND EV'RYTHING IS NORMAL INCLUDING…

KELLY. *(Lightbulb.)* Ooooh.

SAM.

    RIGHT?

KELLY. *(Putting it together.)*

    IF YOU LIKE DON'T PICK UP THE PHONE,
    IT'S <u>SO</u> LIKE NOTHING EVER HAPPENED.

SAM. *(Excitement building.)* Then…

KELLY. Yeah.

> *(Ring.)*

I'M ALIVE!

SAM.

YOU'RE ALIVE!

KELLY. Now that I'm alive, we're doing this senior year my way. Just try to keep up with me, Brown.

OH, WE'RE MOVING ON.

'CAUSE NOTHING ELSE IS STANDING IN OUR WAY.

STAY FOCUSED ON THE PRESENT.

SAM.

WE'RE MOVING FAST.

KELLY.

AND IF IT'S LAME,

WE'RE BLOWING RIGHT PAST.

So what happened first?

SAM. I woke up at Adam's the next morning.

> *(**ADAM** wakes up.)*

ADAM. *(Groggy, lovey.)* Sam, last night was…

> *(**SAM** gets ready to luxuriate in her morning after, but **KELLY** pulls her away.)*

KELLY. Blah blah blah. Kiss kiss kiss. Moving on.

MOVING ON.

SAM.

MOVING ON.

KELLY.

YOU'RE MOVING ON.

SAM.

I'M MOVING ON.

SAM & KELLY.

OH, WE'RE MOVING ON.

> *(**BEVERLY** is lying in wait, arms crossed.)*

BEVERLY. Samantha. Did you have sex?

SAM. Mom. I…um…

KELLY. *(Butting in.)* Did Sam tell you that she picked a college?

BEVERLY. You did?

SAM. I did?

KELLY. Columbia.

SAM. Really?

KELLY. *Broad City.*

SAM. Genius.

BEVERLY. Wouldn't you rather... [go somewhere with trees?]

KELLY.

COLUMBIA.

> *(**BEVERLY** dons Columbia paraphernalia, suddenly totally on board.)*

BEVERLY.

COLUMBIA!

KELLY & BEVERLY.

COLUMBIA!

SAM & BEVERLY.

COLUMBIA!

BEVERLY.

COLUMBIA!

BEVERLY, KELLY & SAM.

ROAR LIONS ROAR!

> *(**BEVERLY** is whisked away.)*

SAM.

OH, I'M MOVING ON.

AND SENIOR PROM IS RIGHT AROUND THE BEND.

KELLY.

YOU'LL NEED A STRAPLESS BRA.

SAM. Duh.

SAM & KELLY.

THEN TO THE SPA!

> *(**SAM** and **KELLY** sit down for pedicures. **ADAM** joins them.)*

PEDICURES FOR THE PROM... ON MOM.
MY TOES ARE GETTING TINGLY.

ADAM.
TINGLY!

SAM & KELLY.
DEE-DEE-DEE-DEE.
WE'RE MOVING ON.

(A disco ball drops. Dance lights flood the stage.)

*(**BEVERLY** enters in an slinky gown. She sings with the band.)*

BEVERLY.
SENIOR PROM
ONLY ONE SENIOR PROM.
IT'S YOUR SENIOR PROM.
BEAUTIFUL LIGHTS,
BEAUTIFUL NIGHT,
RIGHT FOR A SENIOR PROM.
OH OH.
SENIOR PROM.
SENIOR PROM.
OH OH OH!
GLITTERING DISCO BALL.
STREAMERS FALL.
NO, NOTHING LIKE A SENIOR PROM! SENIOR PROM.
SENIOR PROM! OM-OM-OM

*(**SAM** emerges in a prom gown on **ADAM**'s arm.)*

*(**KELLY** appears in a dramatic gown.)*

ADAM. Hey, Kelly.

KELLY. Hey, Adam.

ADAM. Hey... Sting.

BEVERLY. *(As **STING**.)*
"EV'RY BREATH I TAKE"
IS ABOUT HOW PEOPLE WANT TO MAKE OUT,
AND STING MAKES OUT UNTIL DAWN.

(She goes in for a kiss.)

KELLY. *(Ducking.)*

     WE'RE MOVING ON.

SAM. Let's get out of here!

KELLY. Road trip!

     *(**SAM** and **KELLY** jump into the car.)*

SAM.

     WITH KELLY DRIVING, NOTHING'S FATE.

KELLY.

     HOT BOYS, TURN RIGHT. IT'S NOT A DRILL.

SAM.

     HOW DOES SHE NEVER EVEN HESITATE?

KELLY.

     LET'S GIVE THEM A LITTLE THRILL.

     HOW DO YA LIKE THESE?

     *(**KELLY** sticks her ass out the window.)*

SAM.

     IT'S ALL A DREAM.

KELLY.

     ARBY'S!

SAM.

     IT'S ALL SO CLEAR.

KELLY. *(Wielding a sandwich.)*

     GOTTA EAT THIS. CAN YOU STEER?

     *(**SAM** takes the wheel.)*

SAM.

     IN OUR PLAIN...

KELLY. *(Mouth full.)* Oh my God this is amazing.

SAM.

     DULL...

KELLY. Watch out for that semi.

     *(The loud insistent honk of a semi. **KELLY** takes the wheel back.)*

SAM.

> NORMAL,
> GOOD, SIMPLE
> NOTHING MUCH, BEAUTIFUL
> ORDINARY –
> ORDINARY SENIOR YEAR.

> > (**SAM** *dons a cap and gown. She shares a moment of pride with* **BEVERLY**.)

This has been an ordinary senior year for most of us – school dances, a lot of tests, a couple road trips, and some of us even fell in love. But the thing that has made my senior year extraordinary is that I've had my best friend Kelly to share it with.

KELLY & SAM.	**BEVERLY.**	**ADAM.**
OH.	OH MOVING ON.	OH MOVING ON.

SAM.

> WE SAY
> GOODBYE.

KELLY.

SO SAY	OH MOVING ON.	OH MOVING ON.
GOODBYE!		

SAM.

> WE SAY
> GOODBYE TO
> HIGH SCHOOL

KELLY & SAM.

AND FACE THE	MOVING ON.	OH.
WORLD.		
	OH	YOU'RE
		MOVING ON.

SAM.

> THOUGH WE DON'T KNOW
> WHAT WE'LL SEE THERE,   **BEVERLY & ADAM.**
> WE KNOW THAT   OOH
> WE'LL BE THERE.

KELLY & SAM.		BEVERLY & ADAM.
TOGETHER		OOH
IT'S TIME TO		OH
KICK SOME ASS.		

KELLY.

FOR ALL YOU	MOVING
LOWER CLASSMEN,	
SUCKS FOR YOU!	ON.

KELLY & SAM.

PEACE OUT TO	
ALL OUR CREW!	
THE PARTY'S GONE.	MOVING
WE'RE MOVING	

ALL.

ON!

(Ring.)

(The phone rings again and continues to ring.)

*(**SAM** is suddenly back in **ADAM**'s bedroom, waking up.)*

(She answers her phone.)

SAM. Hello? Mom. Don't say anything, I should have come home last night – I know, but...

*(A long pause. **ADAM** tries to brush up against **SAM**. She doesn't react.)*

What?...Well is she OK?...Oh... Oh. Yeah. I'm fine. I'm... I gotta go, Mom... Yeah, I'll be home soon.

(She hangs up.)

ADAM. Are you okay? Sam, whatever it is...

SAM. Don't.

ADAM. Sam...

SAM. Please don't say anything.

(He goes to touch her but she bristles.)

SAM. Please.

> (**ADAM**'s *room disappears. Everything does.*)

> (**SAM** *is alone.*)

["GO TONIGHT"]

> (*A distant phone ring.*)

> (*Slowly, a light rises on* **KELLY** *sitting on the roof of her car.*)

What –

YOU THINK IT'S GONNA BITE?

> (*A distant club groove.*)

KELLY.

> IF WE'RE GONNA GO, WE GOTTA GO TONIGHT.
> GO TONIGHT. GO TONIGHT.
> IF WE'RE GONNA GO, WE GOTTA GO TONIGHT.
> GO TONIGHT.
> GO TONIGHT.

SAM.

> SHE WAS –
> SHE WAS –
> SITTING ON THE ROOF OF HER BEAT-UP CAR
> HALF-SINGING, HALF-LAUGHING, HALF-GOING TOO FAR.
> THE MUSIC PLAYED OVER, WITH NOTHING TO COME.
> IN A REMIX OF MEM'RY, THE LOOP OF THE –
> DRUM
> OR BASS LINE...
> OR WAS IT...

KELLY.

> IF WE'RE GONNA GO, WE GOTTA GO TONIGHT.
> GO TONIGHT. GO TONIGHT.
> IF WE'RE GONNA GO, WE GOTTA GO TONIGHT.
> GO TONIGHT.
> GO TONIGHT.

SAM.

> SHE WAS –
> SHE WAS –

EVERYTHING I'M NOT. MY WHOLE UNIVERSE.
AND I WAS A FOOTNOTE, A SLIM SECOND VERSE.
BUT SHE WAS THE CHORUS,
THE HOOK AND THE GROOVE.
AND WITHOUT HER THERE PUSHING
SOMEHOW I CAN'T –
MOVE.

SO I SIT IN THE CAR THAT SHE LEFT BEHIND
SINKING DOWN IN THIS VOID LIKE A CRATER.
GETTING LOST IN A WORLD THAT I CAN'T REWIND.
IT'S TOO LATE AND IT'S JUST GETTING LATER.

KELLY.

IF WE'RE GONNA GO, WE GOTTA GO TONIGHT.
GO TONIGHT.

SAM.

WHY DID I SAY NO?

KELLY.

IF WE'RE GONNA GO, WE GOTTA GO TONIGHT.

SAM.

WE HAD MILES TO GO.

KELLY.

GO –

SAM.

YOU WERE
MAD TO REACH,
MAD TO DRIVE   **KELLY.**
MAD, MAD   MAD, MAD
AND SO ALIVE.

THE SPACE YOU LEFT,

THE EMPTY AIR

I REACH, REACH   I REACH, REACH
BUT YOU'RE NOT THERE
AND TIME EXPANDS
THE BEAT GOES ON
YOU WERE MAD, MAD
AND NOW YOU'RE –

(Beat.)

SAM.

SHE WAS –
SHE WAS –

SAM & KELLY.

OH

KELLY.

GO

SAM.

OVER AND OVER
YOUR WORDS TO ME ECHO

KELLY.

GO TONIGHT

SAM.

GO TONIGHT

KELLY.

GO

SAM.

OVER AND OVER
AS I TRY TO LET GO.

THERE'S A
BLACK HOLE,
A VACUUM,
IN DEEP OUTER SPACE,
THAT SWALLOWS ALL MATTER
WITHOUT ANY TRACE,
WHERE LIFE IS SUSPENDED
IN PHYSICS AND TIME –
EV'RY WORD YOU SAID HANGS
LIKE AN UNFINISHED –
RHYME.

(Beat. Then –.)

SO I SIT IN THE VACUUM YOU LEFT BEHIND
AND I SIFT THROUGH EACH PHRASE FOR AN EMBER –

KELLY.

GO –

SAM.
FOR A SPARK THAT WILL LIGHT 'CAUSE I CAN'T REWIND.
I UNRAVEL UNTIL I REMEMBER:
SITTING ON THE ROOF OF YOUR BEAT-UP CAR,
WHEN I WAS YOUR ORBIT AND YOU WERE MY STAR.
BUT NOW YOU'RE A BLACK HOLE AND I AM LEFT NUMB
FROM THE LOOP OF THESE MEM'RIES,
THE LOOP OF THE...
THE LOOP OF THE...
THE LOOP OF THE...

(The club beat continues. It stops.)

["YELLOW SUV"]

(Long beat.)

If a yellow SUV is traveling down Elmwood Road at a constant velocity of 57 miles per hour and a pedestrian is crossing the road at 2.5 miles per hour...

If the football player driving the SUV sees the pedestrian from a distance of 132 feet and slams on the brake, decelerating at a rate of 11.1 miles per hour per second, will the SUV still hit the pedestrian?

Yes.

But only if she hears him coming, only if she slows down just enough to look up. It takes two seconds. I *know* that.

What I didn't know was that time *doesn't* stop – prom still has a theme, the valedictorian still gives a speech on a future she knows nothing about.

The truth is I don't remember any of it. Not one slow dance or test. Not one single day of that spring. Nothing woke me up – nothing moved me.

Except one thing...

It was yesterday.

*(**ADAM** appears in the DMV.)*

We were in the DMV. Adam had driven me to take my driver's test. My last ditch attempt before freshman orientation at Columbia. New York City where no one drives.

(The sound of fluorescent lights buzzing.)

ADAM. What number are you?

SAM. Spring had slipped into summer but I was still in a fog, still seeing her everywhere.

(A woman who is not **KELLY** *but is* **KELLY** *walks by.)*

*(***SAM*** stands up and watches her.* **ADAM** *touches* **SAM***'s hand and she comes to – realizes he's there and smiles. She sits down with him.)*

ADAM. Sam?

SAM. Hm?

ADAM. Your number. To take your test?

(He points at the piece of paper she's holding. She looks at it – surprised it's there.)

SAM. 34.

ADAM. How do you feel?

SAM. I don't know.

(To us.) I did know. I felt like real life was the ghost. I felt like the world was passing and I was –

ADAM. I just meant – the test –

SAM. Oh. Good.

ADAM. So, um. I read that book – the one you're always talking about? And it got me thinking. I've been thinking about things a lot – like the idea of, "Everything ahead of me, nothing, nothing behind me..." you know?

(Another **KELLY** *walks by.)*

SAM. I always liked that quote, but it was strange to hear it coming from Adam. Especially now, when I felt the opposite. Everything was behind me.

ADAM. Earth to Sam.

SAM. And all I wanted was to wake up, to snap out of it. I
needed *something* to snap me out of this stupor, this
nothingness.

ADAM. Sam!

SAM. Huh?

ADAM. Sam, I'm trying to say something here.

SAM. *(Snapping to.)* What?

> *(He takes a deep breath.)*

["RUN AWAY WITH ME"]

ADAM.

> LET ME CATCH MY BREATH.
> THIS IS REALLY HARD.
> IF I START TO LOOK LIKE I'M SWEATING, WELL...
> THAT'S 'CAUSE I AM.
> I'M NOT GOOD WITH WORDS.
> BUT THAT'S NOTHING NEW.
> STILL I HAVE TO TRY TO EXPLAIN
> WHAT I WANT TO DO
> WITH YOU...
> WITH YOU –
> RUN AWAY WITH ME.
>
> LET ME BE YOUR RIDE OUT OF TOWN.
> LET ME BE THE PLACE THAT YOU HIDE.
> WE CAN MAKE OUR LIVES ON THE GO.
> RUN AWAY WITH ME.
> TEXAS IN THE SUMMER IS COOL.
> WE'LL BE ON THE ROAD LIKE JACK KEROUAC,
> LOOKING BACK,
> SAM, YOU'RE READY.
> LET'S GO ANYWHERE.
> GET THE CAR PACKED
> AND THROW ME THE KEY.
> RUN AWAY WITH ME.
>
> SAM, I KNOW IT'S FAST.
> I'M IN LOVE WITH YOU.
> SAM, IT'S CRAZY BUT

SAM, I'M CRAZIER FOR YOU.
I HAVE THESE PLANS, SAM,
I HAVE THESE PLANS
OF A HOUSE THAT WE'LL BUILD ON A BAY
WHEN WE RUN AWAY.

LET ME BE YOUR RIDE OUT OF TOWN.
LET ME BE THE PLACE THAT YOU HIDE.
WE CAN MAKE OUR LIVES ON THE GO.
RUN AWAY WITH ME.
ALABAMA HEAT, SIGN ME UP!
WE'LL BE ON THE ROAD LIKE SOME COUNTRY SONG.
WON'T BE LONG.
SAM, YOU'RE READY.
LET'S GO ANYWHERE.
GET THE CAR PACKED
AND THROW ME THE KEY
RUN AWAY WITH ME.

I'M NOT TRYING TO MAKE YOU A WIFE HERE.
I'M NOT TRYING TO TIE YOU DOWN.
I'M JUST SAYING THERE MIGHT BE A LIFE HERE –
A NEW ONE AS SOON AS WE RUN,
RUN AWAY WITH ME.

MISSISSIPPI MUD, WATCH ME SLIDE!
WE'LL BE ON THE ROAD LIKE JACK KEROUAC,
LOOKING BACK.
SAM, YOU'RE READY, SAM.
LET ME BE YOUR RIDE OUT OF TOWN.
RUN AWAY WITH ME.
CALIFORNIA DREAMS, HERE WE COME!
ROMEO IS CALLING FOR JULIET.
READY, SET,
SAM, YOU'RE READY.
LET'S GO ANYWHERE
SAY THE WORD AND I'M ALREADY THERE.
RUN AWAY WITH ME.

    (The moment hangs.)

(CAROL ANN on an intercom somewhere in the distance.)

KELLY. *(As CAROL ANN.)* Number 34.

SAM. Adam –

(What can she say?)

KELLY. *(As CAROL ANN.)* Number 34.

ADAM. That's you.

SAM. What?

ADAM. Number 34. That's you. Go take your test.

SAM. *(To us.)* Kelly said, "Someday a guy will say let me save you. Let me take care of you" and that's when you've gotta –

ADAM. *(Interrupting her thought.)* Hey Sam.

(She turns back to him like Orpheus looking at Eurydice.)

Good luck.

V.

["DRIVE"]

(**SAM** *sits down in an empty car.*)

(**BEVERLY** *sits down in the car seat next to* **SAM**, *who is still lost in her own thoughts.* **BEVERLY** *has a clipboard.*)

(*The test begins.*)

BEVERLY.

OK.

SAM. Mom?

BEVERLY.

BUCKLE UP.

SAM. What are you doing?

BEVERLY.

I'LL BE ADMINISTERING YOUR TEST TODAY.
IF YOU FOLLOW MY INSTRUCTIONS,
YOU WON'T DIE.

SAM. Mom. I don't know what's going on but you have to get out of here –

BEVERLY.

IF YOU FOLLOW MY INSTRUCTIONS,
YOU WON'T FAIL.
DO YOU WANT TO DIE?
DO YOU WANT TO FAIL?

(*She looks* **SAM** *in the eye – it's a real question.*)

SAM.

NO.

(*OK then.*)

(**SAM** *puts her hands on the wheel. The test resumes.*)

BEVERLY.

WATCH FOR TRAFFIC.

SAM.

WATCH FOR TRAFFIC.

BEVERLY.

DON'T FORGET TO BREATHE.

SAM.

DON'T FORGET TO BREATHE.

BEVERLY.

JUST KEEP IT STEADY.

SAM.

OK.

BEVERLY.

RELAX.

DRIVE.

SAM.

DRIVE.

BEVERLY.

SLOW.

SAM.

EYES AHEAD.

FOCUS AND STEER.

DON'T LOOK IN THE REAR VIEW MIRROR.

DON'T THINK.

DON'T SWERVE.

DON'T STOP.

      (**KELLY** *appears with a clipboard.*)

KELLY.

DRIVE.

SAM.

JUST KEEP IT SIMPLE.

KELLY.

DRIVE.

SAM.

KEEP THE SPEED FIFTY-FIVE.

KELLY.

DRIVE.

SAM.

BREATHE AND WATCH THE HIGHWAY.

KELLY.

DRIVE.

SAM.

FOCUS AND DRIVE.

(**KELLY** *takes over the driving test.*)

KELLY.

OK. BUCKLE UP.

SAM. Kelly, stop.

KELLY.

I'LL BE ADMINISTERING YOUR TEST TODAY.

SAM. I have to focus. I have to take this test.

KELLY.

IF YOU FOLLOW MY INSTRUCTIONS,
I CAN FREE YOU.
I CAN MAKE YOU FEEL ALIVE.

SAM.

I CAN DO IT ON MY OWN!

(**BEVERLY** *and* **KELLY** *both bear down on* **SAM.**)

BEVERLY.

EIGHTEEN YEARS HAVE COME AND GONE.

KELLY.

DRIVE.

SAM. *(Trying to focus.)*

DRIVE.

BEVERLY.

EIGHTEEN YEARS YOU'RE MY WHOLE LIFE.

KELLY.

WATCH FOR TRAFFIC.

SAM.

WATCH FOR TRAFFIC.

KELLY.

DON'T FORGET TO BREATHE.

SAM.

DON'T FORGET TO BREATHE.

KELLY.

JUST KEEP IT STEADY. OK.

SAM.

OK. DRIVE.

BEVERLY.

I KNOW MY GIRL.

> *(Then, **ADAM** appears. He takes over the test. A fresh wound, a beating heart. Her mother still hovering – instructing, "helping," making it impossible to focus.)*

SAM.	ADAM.		BEVERLY.
EYES AHEAD FOCUS AND STEER.	OK. BUCKLE UP.		
DON'T LOOK IN THE REAR VIEW MIRROR.	I'LL BE ADMINISTERING YOUR TEST TODAY.		OH, I LOVE –

	KELLY.	BEVERLY.	ADAM.
DON'T THINK. DON'T SWERVE. DON'T STOP.	IF YOU FOLLOW MY INSTRUCT-IONS,	IF YOU FOLLOW MY INSTRUCT-IONS.	IF YOU FOLLOW MY INSTRUCT-IONS,
DRIVE	DRIVE	DRIVE	

ADAM.

I'LL KEEP YOU SAFE.
TAKE THE NEXT EXIT
AND DRIVE.

SAM.

> I DON'T WANT
> TO BE SAFE.

KELLY.

> YOU WANT TO
> TAKE A RISK.

SAM.

> YES.

BEVERLY.

> RISK IS GOOD IF IT'S PLANNED.

SAM.

> I DON'T WANT A PLAN.

BEVERLY.

> CALCULATE THE RISK YOU'RE TAKING.

KELLY.

> BUCKLE UP.

BEVERLY.

> CALCULATE A SHORT EQUATION.

SAM.

> I WANT TO LET GO.

KELLY.	**BEVERLY.**
THE ROAD YOU TAKE SHOULD FEEL RIGHT.	MULTIPLY THREAT
THE ROAD WILL TELL YOU WHO YOU ARE.	BY VULNERABILITY BY COST.

ADAM.

> SAM, YOU'RE READY.
> LET'S GO.
> MAYBE NOT TODAY,
> MAYBE TOMORROW.

BEVERLY.

> I LOVE –

ADAM.

> MAYBE IT'S AS SIMPLE AS
> CALIFORNIA DREAMS.

KELLY.

I LOVE –

ADAM.

ROMEO AND JULIET.

IT'S AS SIMPLE AS THAT.

BEVERLY & KELLY.

(I) LOVE.

ADAM.

SAM, I KNOW IT'S FAST.

I'M IN LOVE WITH YOU.

BEVERLY & KELLY.

I LOVE YOU.

(The music shifts. SAM tries to focus on, not let them get to her.)

SAM. What do I want? What do I need? It doesn't matter if it's a mistake. It doesn't matter if I fail. I have to think big. I have to take control. Even if I disappoint everyone, even if no one ever speaks to me again. I have to feel *something*.

KELLY.

REMEMBER?	**ADAM.**	
	RUN AWAY	
	WITH ME.	**BEVERLY.**
REMEMBER?	IT'S AS SIMPLE	SLOW DOWN,
	AS THAT.	SAM.
REMEMBER?	LET'S GO.	SLOW.

(Their voices build until SAM can't hear herself anymore.)

SAM. Listen to me!

(Silence.)

I NEVER DREAMED OF RUNNING AWAY.

BUT I DO DREAM ABOUT THE HIGHWAY.

I START DRIVING AND KEEP DRIVING.

I CAN'T STOP 'TIL I FEEL ALIVE AGAIN.

FEEL ALIVE ON MY OWN.

AND I WISH I COULD SAY THAT YOU'RE WITH ME,
BUT I KNOW I'M ALONE.

> *(The memory jumble retreats.)*

KELLY.

REMEMBER.

ADAM.

HEY SAM.

BEVERLY.

I WILL LET YOU GO.

KELLY.

REMEMBER.

> *(**BEVERLY** and **ADAM** disappear.)*

> *(A beat. **SAM** looks ahead.)*

SAM.

EYES AHEAD.
FOCUS AND STEER.
DON'T LOOK IN THE REAR VIEW MIRROR.
DON'T THINK.
DON'T SWERVE.
DON'T STOP.

KELLY. You passed.

SAM. What?

KELLY. You got your license. You're ready to go.

SAM. My mom is going to hate me.

KELLY. Maybe.

SAM. And Adam –

KELLY. Yeah.

SAM. I can't do this alone.

KELLY. You're scared.

["I DIDN'T SAY GOODBYE"]

You should be. If you're not, you're not doing it right.

> *(**SAM** doesn't answer.)*

You do it now, you do it for you, and you do it alone. Be mad, Sam. Be careless and wild and squeeze the life out of every second. And don't crash my car. I'm serious. I will, like, haunt you.

SAM. You're the kind of person who would do this, not me.

KELLY.

YOU TAKE THE RISK.
YOU PAY THE COST
YOU DRIVE.
UNTIL YOU'RE LOST.
AND LOOK AROUND.
SEE WHERE YOU WENT.
AND YOUR LIFE
WILL BE A MONUMENT.

SAM. So what – just get the atlas out and – point?

KELLY. What did I always tell you?

SAM. *(A lie.)* I don't remember.

KELLY. Yeah you do.

SAM. "Maps are for brain deads."

KELLY. That's right.

SAM. I didn't say goodbye.

KELLY. Sometimes you don't get to say goodbye.

> *(They look at each other.)*

SAM. I really miss you.

KELLY. I know. It sucks, right?

SAM. Can't we just stay like this?

KELLY. You know we can't.

SAM. Just for a little while longer?

> *(They sit together.)*

> *(Finally, **KELLY** touches **SAM**'s arm. Time to go. She stands up and gives **SAM**'s bag to her.)*

> *(In the background, **BEVERLY** hums.)*

KELLY. What do you want, Sam?

> *(Chord.)*

SAM. I want the deafening sound of driving fast with the windows down.

(Chord.)

SAM. I want to reach the horizon of impossibility.

KELLY.

> I LIVE IN WHAT YOU DO,
> IN WHAT YOU WANT TO DO.
> NOW THAT I'M GONE –

> > *(**KELLY** disappears.)*

SAM.

> I'M MOVING ON.

> > *(**SAM** is alone. She takes a deep breath.)*

> > *(The subtle sounds of suburban life. Sprinklers, cars passing, maybe a lawn mower.)*

> > *(**BEVERLY** enters.)*

BEVERLY. You're up early.

SAM. Oh. I...

BEVERLY. I was watching from the window. I thought you might be cold. But then I thought – well, then she'd get a sweater.

SAM. I am a little I guess.

> *(**BEVERLY** shrugs.)*

BEVERLY. Those are the kinds of thoughts a mom has. But I guess I have to learn how to keep them to myself. I guess it doesn't matter that I don't know why you're out here without a sweater. It doesn't matter that it's cold. What matters – I'm telling myself – is that it's not my call, is it?

SAM. No.

BEVERLY. No. I should probably go back inside.

> *(**BEVERLY** starts to leave.)*

SAM. Mom.

> *(**BEVERLY** turns back. Beat.)*

BEVERLY. Do you remember your first day of school?

SAM. Like ever?

BEVERLY. You were scared you'd do something wrong – like there's a wrong way to be on the first day of preschool.

(*Beat. She's lost in her own thoughts.*)

BEVERLY. The things we do to our girls. What would it look like to let all that go? How could you even – what would it feel like?

(*Beat. She looks at* **SAM**. *A real question.*)

What does it feel like?

(**SAM** *sits down in the car.*)

SAM. Like –

["REMEMBER THIS"]

Like everything in front of you is blank.
It's the first time you've been in the car alone.

(*An intake of air.*)

It's intoxicating. You know what you want but you still haven't turned the key.
You have to savor this – the way it feels to want something so much that you'll risk regretting.
Can you do that?
Can you do something as simple as not know where you're going?
What does it feel like?

(*She takes a deep breath.*)

THE SEAT IS SINKING UNDERNEATH YOUR WEIGHT.
THE SKY IS PALE WITH MORNING LIGHT.
YOUR HEART IS BEATING AT A FASTER RATE.
REMEMBER THIS –
THE RACING HEART,
THE FADED DAWN.
REMEMBER THIS
BEFORE THE MOMENT'S GONE.

SAM & BEVERLY.

THE STREET IS QUIET BUT THE CLOUDS RACE BY,

SAM.

AND WHO KNOWS WHAT THOSE CLOUDS WILL SEE.

SAM & BEVERLY.

BEFORE YOU START REGRETTING,

SAM, KELLY & BEVERLY.

BEFORE YOU TURN THE KEY,

KELLY.

REMEMBER THIS –

SAM.

THE WAY IT FEELS INSIDE THE CAR,

SAM, KELLY & BEVERLY.

THE STILL, COOL AIR.

SAM.

REMEMBER FEELING LIKE YOUR LIFE BEGINS TODAY.

TRY TO STOP AND FEEL EACH SECOND SLIP AWAY.

REMEMBER THIS.

SAM, KELLY & BEVERLY.

REMEMBER...

BEVERLY.

REMEMBER EV'RYTHING THAT LED YOU HERE,

KELLY.

EACH ROAD TRIP AND EV'RY SINGLE TEAR.

SAM, KELLY & BEVERLY.

REMEMBER WHAT YOU'VE LEARNED

SAM.

AND WHAT YOU STILL DON'T KNOW.

SAM, KELLY & BEVERLY.

YOU LOOK BACK ON YOUR LIFE

SAM.

ON THE GIRL YOU WERE FOR EIGHTEEN YEARS.

SAM, KELLY & BEVERLY.

YOU LOOK BACK ONE MORE TIME,

SAM.

THEN YOU LET IT GO.

SAM, KELLY & BEVERLY.

YOUR HAND MIGHT SHAKE AS THE IGNITION LIGHTS.

YOU MIGHT NOT KNOW WHAT ROAD YOU'LL TAKE.
BUT NOW THE GEAR IS SHIFTING.
YOUR FOOT IS LIFTING OFF THE BRAKE.
REMEMBER THIS.

SAM.

REMEMBER
FREEDOM.
FREEDOM.
FREEDOM.

SAM, KELLY, BEVERLY & ADAM.

FREEDOM.
FREEDOM.
FREEDOM.

(Blackout.)

["BOWS"]

End of Show